Houston's had a crush on Dustin since the first time he saw him, even though Dustin was a massive dragon when that happened. Since then, Dustin has shifted back to his human form, and Houston's crush is getting worse. When Houston wants something, he doesn't shy away from trying to get it, and he wants Dustin.

Dustin doesn't understand why Houston is so fascinated with him, but he wishes he'd stop trying to talk to him. He's running from his father, and the last thing he wants is for the clan to find him and threaten the pack.

But Houston knows how to wiggle his way into Dustin's heart, and he does so happily. When Dustin's father finally comes for him, Dustin can't run like he'd been planning to. He didn't expect the pack to stand up for him against his father, but maybe he should have.

Even though it's not enough to stop his father.

Where He Belongs
Copyright © 2023 Catherine Lievens
ISBN: 978-1-4874-3758-9
Cover art by Angela Waters

Published by eXtasy Books Inc

Look for us online at:
www.eXtasybooks.com

Where He Belongs
Mayport Pack 2

By

Catherine Lievens

CHAPTER ONE

Houston looked around, a smile blooming on his face. He liked parties, and he liked pack parties even more. During these moments, the pack truly was like a family, with no infighting and bickering, and he lived for this.

As the beta, it was his job to keep the peace, which he did happily. He'd do pretty much anything for Chance, just like Chance would do anything for him. When Chance had asked him to be his beta, Houston hadn't even thought about it. He hadn't needed to. If his best friend needed his support, he gave it freely.

And he had. They'd been working together for several years now, and Chance was growing into his role. Houston still wasn't entirely sure he had what it took to be a good beta, but he didn't think he was doing too badly, so he wasn't worried about it. His job was to protect the pack and Chance and to keep everyone happy, and he could do that easily enough.

Especially when parties were involved.

Not everyone was there, but then that rarely happened. Some pack members didn't come around for these parties, which was a pity because it was fun. It was also a pity because this party was to welcome Theo and his family to the pack, so it would have been good to have more people to do so.

Unlike James, Houston hadn't been surprised when Chance had fallen in love with Theo. He'd seen it happening and was glad it had. James might not trust Theo and his people, but Houston didn't think they were here to hurt anyone. If anything, they were grateful to Chance for giving them the

1

possibility of having a true pack and being safe.

Houston took a sip of his beer. He could only imagine what they'd gone through. He'd grown up here, with plenty of people to help him when he needed anything. He'd never been hungry and always had a home, but the same couldn't be said for Theo and his family. It was good to be able to give them that, which was why Houston was happy Chance had given them the opportunity to become pack members.

He looked around again, but he couldn't see Dustin. He probably should stay away from the dragon shifter, but he couldn't. He was fascinated by the thought that a normal human could turn into something as massive as a dragon, and he'd always liked fantasy books when he was a child. Meeting a real dragon was a dream coming true, but it would be easier to make that happen if Dustin gave Houston a chance. So far, he'd pushed Houston away and had kept him at arm's length, but Houston hoped the party would change that.

There.

He should have known Dustin would be with his family. It was a minor miracle to see him here at the party since Houston hadn't expected him to come. Wade was eating his weight in pie while he and Theo talked. Dustin hovered close, but he wasn't part of the conversation.

Houston took another sip of his beer, then inched closer. If he wanted to talk to Dustin, he'd have to corner him, and he wouldn't be able to do that if he didn't keep quiet. Dustin would see him coming a mile away, and he'd run and hide.

Houston licked his lips. He shouldn't be as happy as he was at the thought of hunting the dragon, but the fact that Dustin didn't seem to know what to do with him made him want to get to him even more. If Dustin didn't want to talk to him, he'd let go, but the way Dustin reacted to Houston's presence told Houston that he was trying to convince himself and others about that without too much success.

When Houston got close enough, he held his breath and

waited. None of the three men had noticed him, and he could hear them talk.

"I could take him home," Dustin told Theo in a soft voice.

Theo narrowed his eyes at him. He'd been their alpha until they'd become part of the Mayport pack, and they still treated him as such. Technically, Chance was their alpha now, but no one expected them to view him that way so quickly. Theo had been their leader for a long time. It was normal that they still looked at him when they needed something.

"Neither of you is going anywhere. Wade will be fine." Theo didn't sound angry but rather convinced.

Houston almost laughed because he could see the disappointment in Dustin's expression. He'd no doubt hoped Theo would say yes so he could leave the party. Houston's man wasn't a party guy, clearly. He also wasn't Houston's man yet, but Houston was trying to change that.

"I'd still like to go home." Dustin insisted.

Houston didn't blame him. Pack parties could sometimes be a bit much, even for him, and he'd grown up with these people. This party was tame, though. It was nothing more than a family barbecue with beer, good food, and loud music. No one was dancing, and while there would be a pack run later, it wouldn't be too rowdy, since kids would be attending.

"It's important for all of us to be here," Theo told Dustin. "This party is to welcome us into the pack and to show the pack members that none of us is dangerous, not even you. I know you want nothing more than to go back to hide in your bedroom, and I want to let you go, but can you stay a little bit longer? Maybe until the run starts."

Houston wondered if Dustin would go back anyway. His expression told everyone around him that he was unhappy and that he wanted nothing more than to leave, but he still saw Theo as his alpha, and Theo had asked him to stay.

Eventually, Dustin nodded, and Houston breathed easier.

Maybe he'd have a chance to make Dustin see he wasn't a danger tonight. Of course, that would be easier if he wasn't lurking behind Dustin and listening to a private conversation, but as long as no one noticed him, Houston figured he could use all the help he could get with Dustin, including listening to him speak when he didn't think anyone but his family was around.

Dustin was closed off, even from his family. No one knew what had happened to him before he'd found Theo and the others, so there was no way for Houston to understand what was in his past. Whatever it was, it couldn't be good if it had left him feeling like he needed to run away from people.

But the pack was Dustin's home now, and he needed to accept that. Houston hoped he'd be able to. He wanted Dustin to feel at home here and to give him a chance, and that wouldn't happen if Dustin wouldn't even talk to him or look his way.

Since Dustin was staying, it was time for Houston to put his plan into motion. He quickly finished his beer, grabbed a new one, and took a sip of that one, too, to give himself courage. Then, he plastered a smile on his face and moved toward the small group. "Dustin!" he exclaimed so Dustin wouldn't be startled by his sudden appearance.

Houston was vaguely aware of Theo smiling at him, but his entire focus was on Dustin. How could he look at anyone else when Dustin was so handsome?

The first impression someone had when they met Dustin was darkness. His hair was a dark brown that looked almost black and hung in front of his dark eyes as if to hide them. Maybe that was why Dustin wore it so long, or perhaps it was because he hadn't had the opportunity to get it cut yet. Whatever the reason, it suited him and his pale skin. It gave Dustin a gothic look that Houston hadn't previously enjoyed but couldn't stop obsessing over now.

Dustin stared at Houston for a moment. Houston thought he'd turn around and leave, but instead, he nodded curtly. "Houston," he said in a stern voice that sent a shiver down Houston's spine.

Would Dustin sound like that in the bedroom, too? Would Houston ever find out?

Houston was delighted to see that Dustin's cheeks turned a light pink. He didn't look embarrassed, but flustered, and it was all because of Houston. That made Houston want to grab him and drag him into the forest, but instead he just moved closer. He opened his mouth to say something, but before he could, Wade interrupted him.

"Hey, do you know if James has a boyfriend?"

Houston blinked at him, trying to make sense of his words. "I'm sorry?"

Wade looked at him like he was an idiot. "I know you're super busy staring at Dustin, but I was asking if James has a boyfriend."

Why was Wade asking about James? Maybe he was volunteering to get the stick out of James's ass, which wouldn't be a bad thing. "No. He barely ever dates, and it's always a disaster when he does. Why?"

Wade grinned. "Maybe if he were getting laid more often, he wouldn't be so angry at everything all the time."

Houston laughed. He liked the little guy. He liked Dustin more, but Wade had set his eyes on James anyway. Houston didn't understand why, given how uptight James was, but it was none of his business. "Are you volunteering?"

Wade pushed his half-empty plate into Houston's hands. "Why not? At the very least, I'll try talking to him and see what happens."

Houston watched him walk away. The guy had more guts than most people Houston knew.

Dustin looked around, trying to find a way to escape. Maybe if he managed to sneak away from Houston before the man realized he was gone, he'd be able to get back to the house and hide in his bedroom.

But if he did that, Theo would be disappointed, and Dustin didn't want to disappoint Theo. Theo and the others were his family and the only people who cared about him, and even though they were now part of the Mayport pack, Dustin considered Theo his alpha. He had been for a long time, and it would take a while for that feeling to change.

Dustin wasn't sure he wanted it to.

He trusted Theo, but he still wasn't sure about the pack and Chance. He was willing to give them the opportunity to prove him wrong, though. Theo was in love with the alpha, and Dustin wasn't about to take that away from him. Theo and the rest of their small pack deserved to be happy and to put down roots here.

Dustin wasn't sure he'd ever be able to do the same.

He looked around the clearing. Dozens of people were walking around, eating, laughing, and talking. Children ran around the adults, some in their human form, others as wolves. The music was loud, but not so much that they couldn't hear what they were saying, and everyone looked happy.

Everyone but Dustin.

The thing was, Dustin *wanted* to make friends. He wanted to become part of the pack just like Theo, Wade, and the others. But he was terrified and didn't know if there was anything he could do about that. If his father found out where he was, there would be no stopping him, and it would put the Mayport pack and the people Dustin cared the most about in the world in danger.

Dustin couldn't let that happen.

The best way to make sure it didn't was to hide. As long as the word that a dragon shifter was staying here didn't get around, it would be impossible for Dustin's father to find out where he was. The difficulty was that Dustin had an anger problem, and he'd shifted when he shouldn't have. Most of the pack knew about it by now, which meant they were probably gossiping about the dragon shifter who'd moved into their territory and was part of their pack.

They might all be in danger, which was the last thing Dustin wanted. His father and his past were the reasons Dustin had always stayed away from packs. As long as he and his tiny pack had been on the road, squatting and doing what they had to survive, he'd been fine. Now he wasn't sure his luck would hold, but he couldn't find it in himself to tell Theo and the others that he needed to go. He'd rather hide in his bedroom or deep in the forest and still see them from time to time. He'd miss them, but it was best for everyone if he stayed away.

But he hadn't been able to say no when Theo told him to come to the party tonight. It was a pack run, which meant Dustin couldn't participate, at least not in that part of the party. For now, it was nice enough, he supposed. He wasn't used to parties, or rather, he wasn't used to having fun at parties. When his father had held celebrations, it was to put himself and his family at the center of attention, which Dustin loathed.

"So, Dustin," Houston drawled. "How have you been getting on?" He'd put down the plate Wade had handed him on the nearest table.

For a moment, Dustin considered turning around and walking away. He suspected Houston would follow him if he tried that, and since he was at a party, he might as well talk to someone. Houston was pretty easy to talk to, anyway. It could have been worse, like if James had tried talking to Dustin.

Now *that* was a horrifying thought.

"I'm fine," Dustin said. He hoped the short answer would tell Houston he needed to leave him alone. Dustin didn't actually want Houston to stop whatever he was trying to do, but it would be safer. He couldn't allow himself to get close to anyone in case his father found him, both because his father might hurt whoever he was close to and because if he did find Dustin, he'd take Dustin away, and Dustin would lose everyone he cared about.

But his answer made Houston smile more, not less. "That's good to hear. I'm glad you're settling down with the pack."

"Why?"

Houston didn't seem surprised by Dustin's question, even though it was rude. "Why not? You decided to stay, so I want you to like it."

"Do you want everyone here to like it?"

"It's kind of my job as Chance's beta. I'm here to keep the peace and ensure everyone has what they need and want."

"That sounds like an awful job." Dustin was trying to push Houston away, but no matter what he said or how he said it, Houston didn't seem to realize that. Was he as clueless as he was acting, or was he doing that on purpose? Dustin couldn't tell, and he wasn't sure he wished to find out.

For some reason, Houston had decided he wanted to be part of Dustin's life. Dustin didn't understand it, and he was sure he'd regret it, but he kind of liked it. He'd been a pawn in his father's hands for most of his life. His father had never loved him, and he'd only been happy to have Dustin around for what Dustin could get him. Things had been different with Dustin's brother, but they hadn't been close, anyway.

The only people Dustin had ever been close to were Theo and the others, and when they'd reached Mayport, he'd been terrified he'd lose them. He'd been ready to leave them behind because it would have been safer for them and because

8

they deserved a place to call home, but he couldn't stay in one place for too long if he didn't want his father to find him. Theo had managed to convince Dustin to stick around, which was probably a bad idea, but now Dustin was here, and there was no going back.

He supposed that if he wanted, he could sneak out of Mayport territory and get back on the road. Theo and their little family would be distraught, but they'd get over it eventually. Dustin would feel better knowing they were safe, which was all that mattered.

A hand brushed against his, startling him. He looked up at Houston, who was looking down at him with a worried expression.

"Everything okay?" Houston asked.

Dustin wanted to ask why Houston cared but couldn't get his mouth to say the words. It was probably stupid, but Houston's attention made him feel wanted. He knew Theo and the others loved him, but this was different. It looked like Houston wanted Dustin to be part of his life, to *actually* stay, and that wasn't something Dustin had expected from someone he didn't know.

Everyone in Mayport was a surprise Dustin hadn't been expecting. He didn't know what to make of the people here, but he supposed that he'd have to stay if he wished to find out. It might be a stupid idea, but he'd already told Theo he wasn't going anywhere, and he wasn't one to break promises.

Well, except for the promises he made to his father.

There was no way this could end well, but Dustin found that, for once, he wanted to give this a chance. He wanted to be happy, to have the possibility to build a life here, and even though the thought of someone getting hurt was terrifying, as long as he was careful, his father wouldn't find out where he was, and he'd be safe.

Right?

Houston waited for Dustin to answer. For some reason, Dustin seemed spooked, and Houston was pretty sure it wasn't anything he'd done. He suspected Dustin had been thinking about whatever reason had sent him running from his home, and considering how he and the others had been living before they got to Mayport, Houston knew it couldn't be good. He didn't want Dustin to think about that, but he realized there was nothing he could do to make Dustin feel better.

"Dustin?" he asked, gently touching Dustin's arm.

Dustin startled as he had before, but more intensely this time. He took a step away from Houston, his eyes wide as he stared at him. It was almost as if he didn't recognize him, and Houston quickly put down the beer he was still holding and raised both hands.

"It's just me," he said slowly.

Dustin opened his mouth, then closed it again. "I know who you are," he snapped.

"I'm glad you do. I thought I'd lost you for a moment."

Dustin shook his head. "I'm fine."

"Are you sure? Because you don't look fine, and while I realize you don't know me, you *can* trust me. You can tell me what's wrong, and I'll help you."

Dustin stared for a moment before asking, "Why would you do that?"

"Well, you're a pack member now. It means you're my responsibility, and like I explained before, as the beta, my job is to keep people happy. That includes you."

For some reason, Dustin seemed almost disappointed. "You don't have to worry about me."

"Even if I didn't have to, I can't help it. I like you, and I want you to be happy for more than because I'm your beta."

Dustin shook his head and took a step back. "You can't like

me. We barely know each other."

"Then let's talk and allow me to get to know you." Houston could see Dustin was retreating, and he was desperate to keep him here for just a few minutes longer. For some reason, he hoped he'd be able to change Dustin's mind about leaving.

But nothing was ever easy with Dustin, so Houston wasn't surprised when Dustin took another step back and started turning around. "I need to go," he said.

"Then go, but remember that everyone here wants you to be safe and happy. Whatever worries you, we can deal with it together if you tell us."

Dustin hurried away without answering, not giving anyone around him one bit of attention. One of his old pack members tried to stop him, but he brushed her aside. She didn't look confused or offended but sad, which told Houston she was probably used to Dustin treating her and the others that way.

He sighed. Had he pushed too hard and too fast, or was there something else behind Dustin's panic? Because that was how it felt. Houston had been able to see it in Dustin's eyes, and he wished Dustin would tell him what the problem was. He couldn't help if he didn't know. He needed Dustin to realize he was part of this pack and that it meant he wasn't alone anymore. Whoever he needed to fight, he wouldn't fight alone.

"That went well," a voice drawled.

Houston glared at James. He hadn't seen his friend and Wade standing so close, and he wished he had. James would tease him endlessly, and Houston had no patience to deal with that right now.

"Have you lost your touch?" James continued. "I don't think I've ever seen a guy run away from you so quickly."

Wade swatted James's arm. "Don't be rude."

James looked at him with wide eyes. "Why are you still

here and bothering me? I told you to get lost."

"And I didn't listen, because that was rude, too." Wade dismissed James and turned his attention to Houston. "Don't take it personally. Dustin isn't a people person."

Houston smiled at him, because how could he not? "I'm aware of that. I'm not surprised or offended that he ran. I'm just worried."

Wade nodded. "We all are. We thought that Dustin would relax once we settled down here, but it's clear we were wrong."

"You know anything about why he behaves this way?"

"Unfortunately not. He's always been closed off, even with us. He trusts us with his life, but he still won't tell us what he's running from. Every time we ask, he tells us it's safer if we don't know."

"You think he's in danger?"

Wade sighed. "I want to say no, but I can't. The way he behaves hints at that, though, right?"

Houston glanced at the spot where Dustin had disappeared. Dustin running from someone or something would make sense. It would explain why he didn't want to tell anyone and why he either hid in his bedroom at the house his family shared or in the forest. He didn't want anyone to see him, and it was safer and easier if he didn't show his face around. Of course that was only a suspicion, but Houston thought he was right. Whatever had happened to Dustin, it wasn't over, and Dustin was planning on facing it alone.

He wouldn't if Houston had a say in it.

If he wanted to help, he'd have to find out what was going on. He wasn't sure how to do that. There was no way Dustin would tell him if he hadn't even told Wade and Theo. Houston couldn't help but worry. If Dustin was in danger, did that mean the pack was, too? Would whoever was after Dustin tear through the pack to get to him? Houston needed to know, but he had no idea how to find out. If he wanted Dustin to tell him, he'd have to show him he was trustworthy. He wasn't quite sure how to do that when Dustin didn't seem to want to talk to him.

"You think someone is after him?" James asked. His voice was harsh, and his tone told Houston he was about to say something stupid.

Wade squinted. "Maybe."

"And you didn't think to tell us before we accepted you into the pack? Are you putting the pack in danger on purpose?"

Wade's expression turned to anger. "Why are you such an asshole?"

James seemed taken aback by Wade's words. "I'm not an asshole. I just worry about the pack."

"And I worry about Dustin. What do you think will happen if someone is after him and they find him?"

"It wouldn't have been our business if you hadn't become part of the pack."

"Yeah, well, we *are* part of the pack, which means it *is* your business. What are you going to do about it?" Wade snapped as he leaned closer.

They were so close they looked like they might be about to kiss, and Houston couldn't look away. Had James finally found his match? Only a few people stood up to him when he was being an asshole, and James had grown up with those who did. To find someone willing to do the same, even though they barely knew James, was something of a miracle.

Houston had liked Wade before, but right now, he loved him. He was ready to watch Wade kick James's ass, but his mind wasn't far from Dustin.

"I just meant that if someone is after Dustin, we need to be aware of it. I have to keep the pack safe. It's my job, and it's important," James tried to explain.

"Dustin is just as important as your pack. He's one of your pack members, so you need to protect him, too, right?"

"I never said I wouldn't protect him."

"You might not have said it, but I heard the words. You're an asshole." Wade leaned even closer. "I don't know what I saw in you. You're a dick, and I don't need one more of those in my life."

Wade twirled around and stomped away, leaving Houston and James behind. James stared at Wade's back, blinking rapidly.

"What just happened?"

Houston clasped his friend's shoulder. "You were an asshole, and Wade told you exactly what he thought of your behavior."

"I'm just trying to protect the pack."

"Maybe, but you don't need to make enemies within the pack to do that. Wade is right. He and Dustin are pack members now, which means you're supposed to protect them as much as you protect everyone else. You wouldn't have talked to one of our other pack members the way you talked to Wade. You're going to have to grovel if you want to fix things with him."

"There's nothing to fix. We're not even friends."

They might not have been, but Houston hoped James hadn't ruined every chance he had with Wade. James could use a strong guy in his life to tell him when he was being an asshole, and Houston wondered if that guy could be Wade.

Dustin had slowed down as soon as he'd entered the forest. He could still hear the party, people laughing and talking as if they didn't have a care in the world.

They probably didn't. They didn't know what Dustin was running from, and Chance and his father were good alphas.

No one here had to worry about what would happen to them if they didn't follow orders the way Dustin had when he'd been younger. Hell, even though he'd run away from his clan, he still worried about what would happen when his father found him.

He was thirty-two, for fuck's sake. He shouldn't have to obey his father's orders, especially since he wasn't even a clan member anymore. That wouldn't stop his father from trying to order him around, but he'd have to find Dustin before he could do that. Dustin had every intention of staying in hiding until he was sure his father wasn't a danger anymore, which would probably happen when the man died.

Only another twenty to thirty years to go, if Dustin was lucky.

He slowed down, then eventually stopped moving. He wasn't far from the clearing where the party was being held, and he wished he could go back. He didn't understand why, since he'd never been one for parties, but being there, even though few people had talked to him, had made him feel like he was part of the pack. Was this how the others felt already? They didn't have anything to run from or worry about anymore. Dustin did, and he hated his father for making him feel like he couldn't even have this. He'd grown up with the clan, and even though his father was an asshole, the clan had been his home and his family. He'd lost that when he'd left, and he hadn't thought he'd find it again. Now, he might, but he couldn't allow himself to relax.

"Dustin?" a voice called from behind Dustin.

Dustin turned to face Theo. "I'm sorry I left even though I said I wouldn't," he quickly said.

Theo shook his head. "Don't worry about it. This party is overwhelming even for me, and I'm not a loner like you. I'm not here to try to convince you to go back."

"Why not? We're part of this pack now, aren't we? I should

at least stay until the run starts." Not that Dustin would be able to run with the pack. He supposed he could if he stayed in his human form, but in his dragon form, he might end up trampling all over pack members. The last thing he needed was to kill someone.

Theo shook his head. "You don't have to." He hesitated. "But I'd like to know why you're running, if you can tell me. Does it have anything to do with your past? You never told me or anyone else about it, and I worry. I want to keep you safe, but I don't know if I can without knowing what you're running from."

Dustin had been tempted to tell Theo about his father so many times he'd lost count. He'd almost told him but had stopped in time. He didn't want to put Theo in danger any more than he already was.

If Dustin's father found out where he was, he wouldn't let anything stop him from getting him back, including burning the pack to the ground. Dustin wouldn't be able to live with himself if something like that happened.

Besides, what would happen if he told someone about his father? It would be wise for the pack to kick him out before the clan found him. It was what Dustin's father would do if he were in that position. Dustin often wondered if it would be better for everyone if he left, but the thought panicked him. Yes, it would be better if he went far away from the pack, but he didn't have it in himself to leave it behind. He didn't want to be alone anymore. He'd been alone all his life, and he'd believed that was over when he'd found Theo.

But if it was the only way to keep everyone safe, he'd go. He loved these people too much to sit back and watch his father hurt them.

Theo sighed. "You won't tell me, will you?"

"It's better if no one knows."

If it came to it, Dustin would leave without telling anyone.

Telling Theo would just make Theo attempt to convince him to stay or even push him and the others to try going with him. They'd been a pack before, and they wouldn't hesitate to go with Dustin, but he couldn't allow that to happen.

"But we can't help you if we don't know what's going on."

"I'm touched that you want to help, but there's nothing you or anyone else can do."

"You don't know that."

"I do. Look, the people I'm running from aren't nice. If they find out I'm here, they won't hesitate to hurt the pack to get to me." It was useless to act as if someone wasn't after him. He had no doubt that Theo, at the very least, already knew that was the case. "They're not good people, and I won't put you and the pack in danger."

"What if these people find you? What will you do then?"

"I'll leave."

Theo's eyes widened. "You can't leave. We're family. We stay together, remember?"

Dustin did remember. It was what they'd repeated to each other when things were going badly. He couldn't do this to Theo, though.

He stepped forward, putting a hand on Theo's shoulder. "Look, I know you want to help, and I'm touched, but there's nothing you can do. I need to handle this on my own, and if it means leaving the pack, I'll do it. You and the others have found a home here, and I won't take that away from you."

Theo looked like he might be about to cry. "You could find a home here, too."

"I want to. I would if I didn't know who was after me, but I know him well, and I won't put anyone in danger. It's better if this is all you know, and please, don't try to step in. I would never forgive myself if something happened to you."

Theo's expression turned stubborn. "Even if something did happen to me, it wouldn't be your fault. It would be the fault of the person who hurt me."

Logically, Dustin knew that was the truth. Emotionally, though, he'd blame himself if his father attacked the pack.

"I need to go home," he murmured, stepping away.

Theo looked like he wanted to stop him, but he didn't. Dustin had very little control over himself right now. He needed to be careful about what he said before he told Theo something Theo shouldn't know.

Dustin hurried away, keeping an ear out in case Theo came up to him. He was the only one moving, though, but he didn't relax until he reached the house he and the others shared. He ran upstairs to his bedroom, breathing easier only when the door was locked behind him. He pressed his back against the door, as if it would stop his father from coming in and closed his eyes.

When he'd left the clan, he'd believed it meant he'd finally be free of his father. Unfortunately, that wasn't true No matter how much space he put between them, his father was always there, deciding his life. Dustin suspected that would never change, no matter how far and how hard he ran.

He was a prisoner, just like he'd been before, even though his body was free.

And he'd always be one as long as his father was a part of this world.

CHAPTER TWO

The shell Dustin had erected around himself was tougher than Houston had expected, but that wouldn't stop him from trying to break it. He suspected Dustin wanted someone to see through it and give him a chance, but he was terrified of that happening, too. It would be easier to find a way around it if Houston knew why Dustin was so afraid, but unless Dustin told him, he'd have to deal with what he did know, no matter how little that was.

Houston wanted to find out what was wrong. Dustin was the only one in his family who wasn't slowly becoming part of the pack. The others were making friends and getting to know pack members, but Dustin was hiding. Houston understood why, and it might even be the best thing to do depending on why Dustin was doing it, but it didn't mean it was right. Dustin should be able to live his life just like his friends were.

Houston rubbed his face and leaned back against his couch to stare at the ceiling. No matter what he thought or felt, he wouldn't find a way out of this until he found out what had happened to Dustin. The problem was that only Dustin knew, and he wasn't talking. If he never told Theo, there was no way he'd tell Houston, and Houston would have to deal with that.

That didn't mean he was giving up.

He straightened and grabbed his phone from the coffee table, quickly dialing Theo's number. It was the first time he called the alpha mate, but he wanted to know where Dustin was, and Theo probably knew. That way, Houston wouldn't have to wander through pack territory looking for the man he was seeking.

"Houston?" Theo asked when he answered.

He sounded hesitant, which made sense. Even though he and Chance were in love, Theo didn't know Houston or the rest of the pack well yet. Houston hoped he and Theo would eventually become friends because he was one of Chance's best friends, while Theo was Chance's alpha mate. They were both important parts of Chance's life and the pack, and neither of them was going anywhere.

"Hey, I have a question for you," Houston said.

"You do?"

"I was wondering if you knew where Dustin was."

There was a pause before Theo asked, "Why do you think I know?"

"Because you're one of his best friends."

"That much is true, but you know how Dustin is and that he hasn't told me any more than he told you and Chance."

"I know that, but you usually know where to find him. It's nothing bad. I just want to talk to him."

"I'm not sure you'll get anything out of him, but I suppose you might as well try. He's been reacting to you more than anyone else."

"He has?" Houston probably shouldn't be so happy finding that out, but he was. If Dustin had a strong reaction to him, maybe it meant Houston had a chance to get him out of his shell.

"Don't give up on him, please. I don't know how else to help him, and I don't think there's anything I can do that will make him be honest with me. I'm hoping you'll be different."

"I can't make promises, but I'll try. I like him."

Theo chuckled. "I'm aware of that. Well, Wade told me Dustin left early today. He's been in the forest since this morning."

"He's hiding?"

"Probably. Or maybe he's there because he thinks it's safer for everyone else. I hate thinking of him all alone, though. It's not fair."

"I won't drag him out, but I'll try to convince him to come out."

"That's all I can ask for."

"Do you know where in the forest he likes to hide?"

It took Theo a moment to explain, but Houston knew where he'd find Dustin once he did. After all, he'd been born in this forest, and he knew every corner of it. He hung up with Theo and headed out right away, but he hesitated once he was on his porch. Dustin probably wouldn't take it well if he suddenly appeared in front of him, but Houston didn't care too much about that. What he did care about was that he wanted Dustin to understand he was worried about him and wanted him to open up. That wouldn't happen anytime soon, but approaching Dustin in his human form hadn't helped Houston yet. Maybe shifting and doing so as a bear would be different.

Houston quickly undressed and put his clothes into a messenger bag he hung around his neck. He didn't know how long he'd be, so he also texted Chance and James to let them know he'd be in the forest. If they needed anything, they could find him. He then put the phone in the bag so he'd have it with him, just in case.

Once he was done, he shifted, grinning like an idiot. It felt good to be in his bear form and even more so knowing he'd find Dustin and would be able to show off. It might be stupid, but Dustin was important to Houston, even though he didn't understand why or how to deal with the feeling. He'd decided it would be better to accept it and see where things went, but so far, they'd gone precisely nowhere. He didn't blame Dustin, but he still wanted to help.

Being in his bear form meant it would be easier for him to

find Dustin. He raised his nose and sniffed, and while there was a hint of smoke in the air, he was too far away to be able to tell if it had anything to do with Dustin. It did come from the direction Theo had mentioned, though, so he headed that way.

Operation *convince Dustin he was a good guy* had officially begun.

The bag was heavy around Houston's neck, but he was used to moving around the forest like this. Besides, he didn't have to run or attack anyone. It might be annoying, but he'd deal with it if it meant he could get dressed once he found Dustin. He had no idea if Dustin was in his dragon form or in his human form, and he didn't want to make the other man uncomfortable by being naked in front of him. No one in the pack would have cared if Houston had strutted around naked, but Dustin was still a mystery, and Houston didn't want to risk it.

He trotted into the forest, following one of the paths that had been created over years of people passing there. It led deeper into the woods until it disappeared, but Houston didn't need it to know where he was. The smell of smoke grew stronger, so he knew he was on the right track. He pushed on, his bear needing to find Dustin and make sure he was all right.

Being a shifter was an odd thing. Houston and his bear were one and the same, but the bear thought and felt differently sometimes. He acted on instinct more than Houston, and while they usually wanted the same things, the bear had a sweet tooth that was more developed than Houston's. The bear especially liked ice cream, and Houston decided he'd eat some once he was back home.

First, he'd have to find Dustin.

He did. It was impossible not to see Dustin, who was in his dragon form, curled on the forest ground. He'd found enough space that he fit without breaking any branches, but it was tight, and Houston made a mental note to talk to Chance so they could free up some space. Dustin was a pack member now, and he should be comfortable in the forest and with the pack. It wasn't right to ask him to curl up the way he was. He couldn't even move, for fuck's sake.

When Dustin saw him, he huffed, and smoke billowed from his nose. Most people would have run away screaming, but not Houston. Maybe he was an idiot, like James always said, or maybe he knew Dustin would never hurt him. Whatever the reason, he wasn't afraid, and he wasn't going anywhere.

He shifted, quickly grabbed the bag from around his neck, and opened it to take out his clothes. It was cold, so he dressed as fast as he could, even putting on socks. He didn't have his shoes or a jacket, but jeans, a sweater, and thick socks would be enough.

"Hi," Houston said. He sounded a bit out of breath, and it had nothing to do with the run.

Dustin stared at him, his eyes narrowed. He couldn't answer in his dragon form, but Houston suspected he knew what Dustin was thinking. He watched Houston as if he expected him to run away, which was what Houston believed most people would do in his place.

But Houston *wasn't* afraid, and he'd show Dustin that.

Houston was still there, and Dustin didn't understand why. Why wasn't he afraid? The last time Dustin had been in his dragon form in front of a bear, it had been James, and James had freaked out. Houston wasn't, though. He was staring at Dustin with wide eyes and a pleased smile that Dustin couldn't read.

Houston took a step forward. "Theo told me you'd be

around here. Can I touch you?"

Dustin's eyes widened. Had Houston really asked that?

Houston frowned. "Sorry if that was too forward. But you're a freaking *dragon* shifter. You look incredible, by the way."

Dustin wasn't used to anyone complimenting him, especially not when it came to his dragon form. He usually hid it, and back when he hadn't needed to with the clan, there had been no reason for anyone to compliment him. He was just a normal dragon, like everyone else. He wasn't the future alpha like his brother or the alpha like his father. Here, though, he was different, and he wasn't sure he liked it.

But he did like the way Houston's eyes glittered when he looked at him. There was no fear or disgust in his gaze. He almost vibrated with what Dustin thought was anticipation. He supposed he didn't have to understand why Houston was so excited. Houston wanted to touch him because he was fascinated, nothing more, nothing less.

He stared for a moment longer as Houston waited, one hand lightly raised as if he were about to touch Dustin. Dustin had no doubt that Houston would drop his hand and step away if he said no. He wasn't sure the other man would leave him completely, but he didn't want to be alone.

Even though he was surrounded by people every day, Dustin was lonely. It came from having to hide and being unable to be honest with the people surrounding him. He didn't know if there was a way out of it, but Houston soothed that feeling, and Dustin clung to that. Houston would go back to his life eventually, leaving Dustin alone once again, but Dustin would deal with that when it happened. For now, Houston wanted to touch him, and he wanted to be touched.

He couldn't remember the last time someone had petted him while he was in his dragon form. It had probably been his mother, and it hadn't happened since he was a child. His father wanted his sons to be thick-skinned and not need affection, but it didn't work that way, at least not for Dustin.

Still staring at Houston, he slowly nodded. There was barely any space between the trees for him to move, even just his head, but it was worth seeing the delight in Houston's expression. He stepped closer and gently touched the tip of Dustin's nose.

When Dustin didn't push him away, his touch became bolder and stronger. He stroked Dustin's nose, then up to his forehead, and Dustin closed his eyes in pleasure.

He'd missed this so much. Even though Theo and the rest of their ragtag family accepted him, it was different for Houston to do the same. Theo, Wade, and the others were Dustin's *family*. Houston was little more than a stranger, yet he'd welcomed Dustin into the pack and was doing everything he could to make Dustin feel like he belonged.

"This is incredible," Houston murmured as he continued stroking.

He moved to Dustin's cheek, gently tickling it until Dustin huffed. That made Houston laugh.

"You're much warmer than I expected, although I should have known," Houston said. "You're a dragon, after all. But I've never met a dragon shifter before, so I don't know much about you and what's normal for you. Hopefully, that'll change soon."

Dustin frowned. Houston wanted to learn more about him, and while Dustin wasn't afraid Houston would use whatever knowledge he found against him, he didn't understand the man. Dustin had been trying to keep him at arm's length like he had with everyone else, but Houston kept pushing back. He was the only one, and something told Dustin he wasn't giving up. It wasn't in his nature, and Dustin had no idea how to deal with that.

Maybe he didn't *have* to push Houston away. He wanted

to keep the pack safe, but surely, Houston wouldn't be telling anyone about what was happening right now. He wasn't an idiot. He knew better than to tell people about Dustin being a dragon shifter. He also didn't strike Dustin as being the kind of person who spread gossip, although Dustin didn't know him that well.

But maybe having one more person in his life that he could trust wouldn't be the disaster Dustin expected. Of course, he couldn't tell Houston about his father any more than he'd told Theo, but hopefully, Dustin could trust him with everything else.

Houston was still stroking Dustin, but he moved on to his side. He was telling Dustin about the pack members, how they were related, and funny stories about some of them. He was telling Dustin about the pack to make him feel like he belonged, and it was working.

Dustin closed his eyes and let Houston's voice soothe him.

Then Houston's words snagged Dustin's attention.

"I mean, I don't know about you, but if I could stay home all day and watch TV and play around, I would, but everyone needs a job, right?" Houston said as he scratched behind Dustin's ear. "No one is trying to rush any of you guys, though. I also know you won't be comfortable with having a job in town, so maybe we can find you something in pack territory."

Of course. Chance had been clear that if he allowed their pack to stay, they'd need to make themselves useful. He wanted them to have jobs and contribute, which was why Houston was here. Instead of doing that, Dustin had been hiding out in the forest, and it was time for him to get a move-on.

But what was he supposed to do? He didn't want to work in town and was thankful Houston understood that. Still, Dustin was a bit disappointed that Houston had found him for that and not because he wanted to spend time with him.

He should have known better. No matter how fascinated Houston was, Dustin was still just a guy.

"And I think having a job would help you feel even more part of the pack," Houston was saying. "Even if it's something small. Theo and the others are integrating into the pack and starting their lives, but you're not, and I feel sorry about that. I just want to help you in any way I can. Maybe a job would, or maybe we'll have to find something else." Houston's eyes widened, and he smiled. "You know what else would help you feel part of the pack? Going on a date with me."

Dustin blinked, trying hard to make sense of the words. He wanted to ask Houston what he meant, but he'd have to shift to do that, and he wasn't ready for that. Hopefully, Houston would explain without Dustin having to prompt him.

"Have you been in town yet? I mean, since your pack arrived? It would be a great idea and an honor for me to take you on a date and show you around."

Dustin didn't understand why Houston would consider it an honor, but there was so much he didn't understand about Houston. Maybe he should stop trying and just bask in the attention and affection.

Because it was clear that Houston liked Dustin. Dustin hoped it wasn't just that he was a good actor, especially since he liked Houston, too.

"So? What do you think? Want to go on a date with me?" Houston asked.

Dustin couldn't answer like this, so he decided to shift. He couldn't leave this spot without doing so, anyway. He might as well do it now so he could say yes to Houston's offer.

He focused on his human form, and his body started shrinking. Houston stayed where he was, and by the time Dustin was back in his human form, Houston's hand was pressed against his chest.

They stared at each other. Houston was dressed, while

Dustin was completely naked, and Houston's hand was on him.

Dustin swallowed. Maybe shifting hadn't been a great idea, after all.

Houston hadn't expected Dustin to shift, which was the only explanation he had as to why he was touching Dustin's chest. He snatched his hand away, but he was grinning like an idiot. "Sorry about that. I would have stopped touching you if you'd warned me you were about to shift."

Dustin glared at him. "How could I warn you if I couldn't tell you?"

He didn't wait for an answer and turned around, apparently looking for something. Houston understood what that something was when Dustin stepped closer to one of the trees he'd been leaning against and reached up for a bundle of clothes. He quickly put them on just as Houston had minutes earlier, carefully avoiding looking at Houston.

Houston was still waiting for an answer. He knew he was taking a risk when he'd suggested he and Dustin could go on a date, but he didn't regret it. Either Dustin said yes, or he didn't. Whatever his answer would be, Houston would deal with it.

But Houston couldn't stop smiling. He'd been anticipating being allowed to touch Dustin's dragon form, and it had been everything he'd dreamed of. He'd known about dragon shifters before, but as far as he knew, there weren't many of them around. He'd certainly never met one, which explained why he was fascinated. He was glad Dustin had allowed him to pet him, but it was clear the moment was over, and Houston wondered what would come next. Would Dustin tell him he didn't want to go on that date?

Houston wouldn't be surprised if that was the case, and he

wouldn't blame Dustin. It was a lot to take in, and Dustin was still dealing with whatever he was hiding.

"Why?" Dustin eventually asked.

Houston had purposefully been looking away while he dressed, but now, he turned to him. Dustin's cheeks were flushed, and he was still putting his shoes on, carefully avoiding Houston's gaze.

"Why what?" Houston asked.

"Why do you want to go on a date with me?"

"Why wouldn't I want to go on a date with you?"

Dustin glared. "You can't answer my question with another question. You don't know me. The only things you know about me is that I'm hiding and that I can turn into a dragon."

"And that's not enough to want to take you on a date?"

Dustin stared, clearly waiting for Houston to give him an answer.

If Houston was honest with himself, he wasn't sure why he was so eager to get to know Dustin. He was fascinated and wanted to help Dustin, but was that a good enough reason?

He decided to be honest. If he wanted Dustin to be honest with him, he needed to do the same. "Right now, I'm fascinated by you. It has a lot to do with the fact that you're a dragon shifter, sure, but that's not the only reason. You're an incredibly handsome man, and you make me curious. I want to know you better and see what you're hiding under your shell, and the only way for me to do that is to get to know you. What better way than going on a date?"

Houston wasn't surprised that Dustin was asking why he wanted to take him out on a date. He'd been hesitant since the beginning, convinced the pack wouldn't see anything important in him and that they'd kick him out. He seemed to have low self-esteem, and Houston didn't know why. Maybe it had to do with what Dustin was hiding. Whatever it was, he doubted Dustin would be comfortable with telling him. That was fine with him, at least for now. Eventually, he'd find out what was wrong and try to fix it if Dustin allowed him to.

But first, he had to convince Dustin that doing this was a good idea. He wanted Dustin to want to go on a date with him as much as he wanted to go on a date with Dustin.

"You don't have to take me on a date to get to know me," Dustin said. "Besides, friends don't go on dates."

Did Dustin truly not understand, or was he trying to tell himself that Houston only wanted friendship from him?

Until now, Houston had tried to tone things down. He didn't understand why he was so attracted to Dustin and so eager to have him in his life, but he didn't care. He just cared that he wanted Dustin and that it looked like Dustin wanted him but, for whatever reason, was too afraid to say yes. He was trying to convince himself that all of this was too good to be true, and Houston wanted that to change. He wanted Dustin to see himself the way Houston saw him, to understand how fascinating he was, and not only because he was a dragon shifter. Sure, Houston was excited about that, but it was nothing next to how he felt about Dustin, the man.

Houston leaned closer. Dustin's eyes widened, but he stayed where he was, which was good because Houston wanted them to be close. Houston heard Dustin's breath hitch, and while he wanted nothing more than to kiss Dustin, he kept his lips to himself. Still, he wanted Dustin to understand why he was so interested in him.

"Who said I only wanted to be friends with you?" he asked with a purr.

Dustin blinked rapidly. "What else could you want?"

"If you don't understand, then maybe I'm not doing my job correctly."

That startled a laugh out of Dustin. "I don't think your job as a beta includes trying to date people."

"Nor does it include trying to convince them they're worthy of dating. But you are, and I want to spend time with you."

Dustin shook his head. "I just don't get it."

"You don't have to. Emotions don't always have a reason. They just are. In the beginning, it was fascination because you're a dragon shifter. After talking to you a few times, I think I prefer your human side."

"You can't know that."

"That's what you think, but I'm convinced of the opposite. Even so, I'd like it if you allowed me to show you that I do care about you. Let me take you on a date. Let me show you that I really want you and, even more importantly, that you're home here. You need to accept that and let go of the fear. Whatever happened in your past, there's no way it's as horrible as you think."

"That's not why I never told anyone," Dustin whispered. "I didn't do anything wrong, or at least not something that most people would view as wrong."

Houston took a chance and reached for one of Dustin's hands. Dustin stared as if he wasn't quite sure what Houston was doing, but he didn't stop him when Houston linked their fingers together. "In time, I hope you'll trust me and that you'll be comfortable enough to be able to tell me. In the meantime, I don't care what you're hiding or what happened to you beyond the fact that it brought you here. I know you think you're protecting the pack, and maybe you are. Who's going to protect *you*, though? Who's going to be there for you and support you when you need help?"

Dustin looked away. "I have Theo and the others."

"And that's great. But *I* want to be there for you, too. I want to show you that more people care about you than you think, and that whatever happens, we won't give up on you. It doesn't matter if you hide in the forest for weeks or months.

The pack is your home whenever you feel ready to accept it."

Houston had said everything he wanted to stay, and now it was time for him to give Dustin time and space to digest all of it. He took a step back and tried to let go of Dustin's hand, but Dustin clung on. The gesture sent Houston's heart racing, and he wondered what it meant.

He didn't have to wonder for long. Dustin turned toward him, and Houston didn't think he'd ever seen his eyes so wide. There was a well of emotions there, and Houston wished Dustin would trust him with them.

"All right," Dustin said.

Houston was lost for a moment. "All right?"

"I'll go on a date with you."

Dustin wasn't sure why Houston looked so shocked. He'd asked him out, after all, so what had he expected? Dustin didn't understand Houston, but he was getting excited about the thought of discovering him. He wanted to understand Houston, which wasn't something he often felt. It was terrifying, and he didn't know if he'd be able to make himself vulnerable, but for the first time in forever, he was willing to try. Surely, that had to mean something.

Then Houston beamed. He looked as if Dustin had handed him the world, and his reaction made Dustin smile, too.

Houston talked, starting to drag Dustin away. "Let's go."

"Where?" Dustin asked, looking around. He'd been here to hide, but Houston clearly wouldn't allow him to continue doing so.

"You just said you'd go on a date with me, so let's go."

"I didn't mean right now," Dustin complained.

"I'm not going to take the chance that you'll change your mind. We're going on a date, and we're going now."

Dustin laughed. He almost didn't recognize himself. He

was still afraid his father would find him and that he'd put the pack in danger, but for once, that was easy to ignore in the face of the excitement brought on by Houston. Surely one date in the small town wouldn't hurt. Surely Dustin's father wouldn't find him here.

But Dustin was starting to see he wouldn't be alone facing him. Even if the rest of the pack stayed back, Houston wouldn't. He cared about Dustin, even though Dustin didn't understand why, and he'd be there for him. He wouldn't be the only one, and Dustin had never felt so strong.

He wasn't alone anymore. He hadn't been alone for a long time, but he hadn't allowed himself to see that. Now that he did, he knew he could face his father.

But he'd really rather not.

Houston didn't seem to care that he didn't have shoes as he pulled Dustin along. Dustin had his and even a jacket, but they had to stop at Houston's house so he could finish getting dressed. They were taking Houston's car, anyway, and as Dustin waited on Houston's porch, he started getting nervous.

Thankfully, Houston seemed to be able to read Dustin. He was out of the house in just under ten minutes and pulled Dustin to the car. He even opened the door for Dustin, which made Dustin roll his eyes, but he couldn't deny he enjoyed it.

Theo and the rest of Dustin's ragtag family cared about Dustin. Dustin was aware of that, and he loved them for it. This was a different kind of care, though. Houston saw Dustin as a man, and he wanted him. He wanted to keep him safe and happy, and that wasn't something Dustin was used to. He wasn't quite sure how to deal with it or how to behave, but he supposed that going on a date with Houston would be a good first step. He had no idea what would happen during the date or after it, but for the first time since he'd arrived in Mayport, he was excited to find out.

"Where are you taking me?" he asked as Houston drove.

He was only half surprised at how messy the car was. It wasn't dirty, but there were three empty bottles of water in the backseat, a sweater, several packs of chips, and one lone shoe. It was nice to see that Houston wasn't perfect, even though Dustin knew that already.

The town of Mayport was so close to pack territory that they could have walked. Maybe they would have if it hadn't been so cold. Dustin enjoyed being in the car with Houston, though. Houston had turned on the radio, and he was humming along with the songs. It was soothing, and it gave Dustin the impression of the familiarity they didn't yet share. He could see them doing this for years to come, and the thought made his heart beat faster.

"To get ice cream."

Dustin frowned. "It's too cold for ice cream."

Houston gasped. "It's never too cold for ice cream."

Dustin wasn't sure about that, but he supposed he could give it a try. It would make Houston happy, and for some reason, Dustin *wanted* Houston to be happy.

Houston parked in the grocery store parking lot and rushed around the car. Dustin was already out by the time Houston reached him, but Houston didn't seem disappointed. He took Dustin's hand and dragged him away, and Dustin decided to just go along with it and see what happened.

It was odd for him to be outside of pack territory, and he looked around. He'd stayed hidden even in the first days after he, Theo, and the rest of their pack had arrived, and he hadn't seen much of it.

It was tiny, but there was everything one might need. He saw the grocery store where they'd parked, a diner, a coffee shop, a bakery, a store that seemed to sell wooden furniture, and even a pet store. Further down the street was a mechanic and what looked like a daycare. From what Dustin knew, almost everyone who lived and worked in Mayport was a pack member, and the few people who weren't were human. Knowing that made him feel safe and allowed him to relax.

Houston turned a corner, and Dustin saw a big park. A few children were playing around, dressed in heavy coats and hats. Right in front of the park was an ice cream parlor, and Dustin wasn't surprised that was where Houston dragged him.

It was quaint and well-illuminated, but Dustin still shivered at the thought of having ice cream in the cold. He was ready to give it a try, though.

"Now, this is the most important question," Houston said as they walked in. "What will you choose?"

There were many choices, and it was overwhelming. Dustin decided on two—salted caramel and white chocolate. He wasn't sure if Houston approved of it, but the other man didn't say anything as he selected four different flavors and paid.

They sat by the window, and the place was warm enough that Dustin took off his jacket. The ice cream was good, and he was hungry, so he found himself devouring it.

"So you see, Chance, James, and I have always been close," Houston was saying. "They grew up in my house, and I grew up in theirs. We were inseparable when we were younger, and we still are. No one was surprised when Chance asked James and me to be his beta and head of security when he became alpha. You should have seen how happy my parents were. I guess they'd never really thought about it."

"What about siblings?" Dustin asked. He was curious about Houston's life, and a date was meant for them to get to know each other, right?

Houston shook his head. "I don't have any. I'm an only child, although I guess that considering how close I am to

35

Chance and James, it was like having brothers. What about you? Do you have siblings?"

Dustin swallowed. "A brother."

Houston seemed surprised Dustin was willing to admit that. "Older or younger?"

"Older." That was all Dustin could tell Houston about Mark. He didn't want to risk it.

Thankfully, Houston seemed to understand that. Dustin suspected he wanted to push, but he didn't.

"Well, you'll make enough friends here not to have to worry about having siblings," Houston said.

"How can you be so calm?" Dustin blurted out.

Houston blinked. "About what?"

"You don't know anything about me. It's clear I don't want to tell you about my past, but you don't seem worried. I could be hiding something, like maybe I'm a serial killer, and you don't seem to care."

Houston laughed. "You're not a serial killer. I don't think you have it in you to kill anyone. But I *am* curious. I'd pay you if I thought it would make you tell me about your past, but it's clear that whatever happened to you, you're not over it, and you're terrified. I'm not going to send you running just because I can't be patient."

"But you're the beta. This might be dangerous. *I* might be dangerous."

"I don't think you are." Houston took Dustin's hand over the table. "And if someone is after you and it's dangerous for the pack, I trust you to tell me."

But Dustin hadn't told Houston. He hadn't told anyone. He might be putting the pack in danger right this moment, and he didn't know how to make Houston see that without having Houston reject him. "The pack might be in danger," he murmured.

"Then we'll deal with it together. Is it going to happen

anytime soon?"

"I don't know. I've been trying to hide so they won't find out where I am."

Houston nodded. "Then you continue doing so, but maybe you don't have to hide while you're in pack territory. You can spend time with your family, or even with me. I want to be there for you, Dustin."

"Why?" Dustin could hear the desperation in his voice, but he needed an answer.

"Because I can see my future in you. Whatever happened to you, whoever is after you, will not change the fact that I want to be with you."

He leaned even closer and pressed their lips together. Dustin's heart stuttered, and for a moment, he was stunned and unable to think. Houston started moving back as if he was afraid Dustin hadn't wanted him to kiss him, but there was nothing further from the truth. Dustin pressed closer and opened his lips to Houston. Houston's tongue swiped in, cold and tasting of chocolate and mint.

And of home.

CHAPTER THREE

Houston whistled as he went over his to-do list for the day. It got him a glance from James, and Houston could see the questions on his face. He ignored him, knowing that if James wanted something, he'd ask.

Sure enough, only seconds later, James put down his phone. "What are you so happy about?"

Houston grinned at him. "The sun is shining, and I have coffee. Why shouldn't I be smiling?"

James's eyes narrowed. "This isn't like you."

"I'm always happy."

"Yes, but not like this. What did you do?"

Houston pressed a hand to his chest. "Why do you think I did something? Don't you have any faith in me?"

"I don't trust you as far as I can throw you. What did you do? Am I going to have to deal with the outcome?"

Houston rolled his eyes. James had always been a bit uptight, but since Chance asked him to become head of security for the pack, it had become worse. James took his work seriously, which was good, but he seemed to believe that the pack would burn to the ground if he wasn't on guard twenty-four hours a day, seven days a week.

"You won't have to deal with anything," Houston reassured him. "And if you really want to know, I'm happy because Dustin and I are dating."

Houston didn't have to look up from his list to see James gaping at him. He knew his best friend. James would start asking questions if he stayed silent. He might believe gossip was beyond him, but he was always the first to ask questions.

Today wasn't any different.

"Dustin? You mean the dragon shifter?" James asked, his voice slightly strangled.

"Do you know another Dustin?" Houston answered, finally looking up.

James was behind his desk, staring. Houston had his own office, but he didn't like working by himself. He'd much rather have someone else in the room making noise so he'd feel less lonely. When he couldn't work with James or Chance, he usually put on some old TV show he didn't have to focus on. It gave him the impression someone was in the room with him.

"You can't be serious. You're dating the dragon?"

Houston leaned back against the couch. It wasn't particularly comfortable because it was old, but it was better than having to sit on the floor. "Why did you say it like that?"

"Because I can't believe it. He's dangerous, Houston. You can't do things like this."

"Why? Besides, he's *not* dangerous."

"He attacked me."

"Only because you were being an asshole. You provoked him. *You* are the one who told me that, so don't try sniveling your way out of this."

"I needed to see what we were up against, and now I know. You can't afford to trust him."

Houston was getting angry. He was sure James was worried about him, but it didn't give him the right to say these things about Dustin. "Stop talking about him as if he's a rabid animal. You might not like him, but it doesn't mean you can insult him."

"It has nothing to do with liking him. He could burn this pack to the ground. He could kill dozens of people just by shifting at the wrong moment."

"And you could kill someone by having a tantrum while you were in your bear form. It doesn't mean people stay away from you, so stop it, all right? Dustin isn't going to hurt anyone. Yes, he reacted badly when you provoked him, but you knew he had an anger problem."

"Exactly. What's going to happen if he gets angry at the wrong moment?"

"If he does, we'll deal with it. I won't give him a reason to be angry, though, so stop freaking out."

But James was already shaking his head.

Houston had known his friend wouldn't be happy to find out he and Dustin were dating, but this was one of the times he didn't care what James thought. James would have to wrap his mind around it and get used to it, and that was that. Houston wasn't giving up on Dustin just because James didn't like him and thought he'd eat him for breakfast.

Thankfully, the phone on James's desk rang. He looked down, then back up at Houston. His expression told Houston their conversation wasn't over, but if Houston was lucky, he'd be out of the house before the phone call was over.

"Don't go anywhere," James snapped. "It's Chance."

Houston groaned. "I don't have to wait. If he's calling you, there's a reason, and it probably has nothing to do with me."

James pointed his finger at Houston in a silent order, and Houston sat back. Yes, he could leave, but James would come after him. He might as well stay here and see what was happening.

"Chance," James said when he answered.

Houston couldn't hear the other side of the conversation from where he was, but that didn't last long. James frowned, lowered his phone, and touched something on the screen, putting it on speaker.

"Can you repeat that? Houston is here with me," he said.

"Why aren't you answering your phone?" Chance asked.

Houston looked around, trying to locate it, but he couldn't see it anywhere. "I don't even know where it is."

"Well, you have to find it, but not now. You're needed at the diner."

Houston got to his feet, and his phone clattered to the floor. He still had no idea where it had been, but at least he'd found it. When he checked it, he wasn't surprised to see it was off. The battery had probably died.

"Why am I needed at the diner?" he asked.

"There's someone there looking for the alpha."

Houston and James exchanged a glance. People didn't go around looking for alphas just because they felt like it. Whoever this was had to have a good reason to want to talk to Chance. "You want me to find out who they are and what they want before I call you?"

"Yes. I'll be on standby if you need anything, but it would be great if you could tell me what's happening. I'd go myself, but Theo is worried it has to do with his people."

Houston's eyes widened. Dustin was running from something, and someone had just appeared at the pack's door looking for the alpha. Could the two things be related?

Houston wouldn't find out until he talked to whoever was at the diner, so he needed this conversation to be over. "I'll call you as soon as I know more," he promised.

"See that you do. Theo is nervous, and I don't like it."

James stayed behind, even though Houston knew he wanted to come along. His job was to protect the pack, and he was always anxious when something out of the ordinary happened. His place right now was in pack territory with Chance, though.

Houston rushed out, relieved to have a battery pack in his car. He hooked up his phone before driving out of pack territory so he'd be able to call Chance once this meeting was over. When he reached Mayport, he parked close to the diner, grabbed his phone even though it wasn't charged much yet, and made his way to this impromptu meeting.

Alice, one of the waitresses, met him at the door. She kept looking back to a table where two men were sitting, drinking coffee and quietly talking.

"Did they say who they are?" Houston asked in a whisper, leaning closer.

She shook her head. "No, and I didn't ask. They just asked if there was any way to contact the alpha, and I told them I'd take care of it."

"You did the right thing. Chance sent me."

"I didn't know what else to do."

"I'll take care of it. Keep everyone away from the table, all right? I don't know who they are, and I don't want to risk it."

"You think they're dangerous?"

"I don't know. I don't want to take the risk."

Alice nodded, hesitated, then quickly said, "They smell like Dustin."

Houston blinked. "What do you mean?"

"Dustin, the dragon shifter? I was close to him for a bit at the party the other week, and I was able to smell him. I was curious because he's a dragon shifter, and I wanted to know if I'd recognize him by scent. These guys smell of smoke like he does."

Houston peered at the two men again and swallowed. They might just be dragon shifters. How had Houston gone from never meeting one to meeting too many of them? He only needed one dragon shifter in his life, and that was Dustin.

But they were here, and they wanted to talk to Chance. It was Houston's job to find out why.

He made his way to the table, stopping next to it.

"Gentlemen," he said.

The two men looked at him. One of them was younger,

probably in his thirties, while the other looked to be in his six-
ties, if not older. That one's hair was completely white, but
not enough to hide the resemblance between the two. Houston had no doubt he was in front of father and son.

"Who are you?" the older man asked.

"My name is Houston, and I'm the Mayport pack beta. My
alpha sent me since he's busy at the moment."

The man frowned and opened his mouth, but the younger
guy spoke before he could say anything. "I'm Mark, and this
is my father, Earl. He's the alpha of our clan."

"We're here to take Dustin back," Earl cut him off. "Hand
him over, and we'll go without burning this town to the
ground."

Dustin stared at his bedroom ceiling. He was hiding, but it felt
different from before.

After he and Houston had gone on their first date and got
ice cream, they'd seen each other several times. It wasn't always easy for Houston to find a moment to spend time with
Dustin, especially since Dustin was still wary of leaving pack
territory, but they were dealing with it. There had been more
kisses, many hugs, and a bit of fumbling in the back of Houston's car, and it was everything Dustin had never thought he
could have.

When he'd left the clan, he'd known he'd have to be alone.
It was too dangerous to start dating or make friends when his
father could find him at any moment. Over the months,
though, Dustin had come to realize he couldn't be on his own.
If he'd insisted on going that way, he'd probably be dead in
an alley somewhere. He'd let Theo in, then the others, and
now Houston.

It was still dangerous. There was a chance that Dustin's father would find him, and if that happened, Dustin would

have to run. He'd do it because it would mean keeping his family safe, but he'd really rather not. He was getting used to living with the pack, finally relaxing, and the thought of losing everything terrified him.

That was why he was still staying out of sight when he wasn't with Houston. He hadn't been spending as much time alone in the forest, though, and the others had noticed. Wade kept staring at him and smiling while Theo had asked a few pointed questions Dustin hadn't answered. He wasn't going to, either. For now, he was happy to keep Houston and what they were doing a secret. He wanted to savor it for a bit longer without anyone sticking their noses into their budding relationship.

But that was what Dustin and Houston had, wasn't it? They were dating, which meant they were in a relationship. Dustin liked Houston more than he'd expected, and he liked him more every time he found out something new about him. Houston was the pack's beta, and he was strong and opinionated, but he never pushed Dustin into doing something he wasn't ready for or didn't feel comfortable with. Dustin wasn't an idiot, and he knew that most guys would have already wanted sex by now. Houston hadn't even hinted at it. He seemed content to take Dustin out to the ice cream parlor, for a walk in the park, or even to the movies a few towns over.

Houston hadn't even asked much about Dustin's past. He knew Dustin was hiding something and that someone was coming after him, but he hadn't demanded an explanation. Dustin felt guilty because he was putting the pack in danger, and he wouldn't be able to avoid telling Houston and Chance for much longer, but it felt nice to forget that his father had been hunting him for a while. It had been a long time since Dustin had truly felt safe, and he didn't want to lose that feeling.

His phone vibrated on the bed next to him, and he quickly

snatched it up, smiling when he saw Houston was calling. He was always smiling when it came to Houston, and he couldn't see himself stopping anytime soon.

"Hello," he said when he answered.

He and Houston had been calling each other every day, several times a day since their first date. Even when they couldn't find the opportunity to spend time together, they were never far from each other. Houston called to tell Dustin what he was doing, about his day, or to ask him where he was. He was just checking in, but it made Dustin feel cherished and like he mattered.

Maybe he *had* found a new home in the end. Maybe he'd be able to stay here and make a life in Mayport. He was afraid to hope, but he couldn't stop himself from doing just that.

"Where are you?" Houston asked.

Something in his voice made Dustin frown. He sat up, trying to pinpoint what it was. "In my room. Why?"

"Something happened."

Dustin turned cold. "What?"

"I was called to the diner. Someone there was looking for Chance, and he sent me to find out who it was. Your father and brother are here, Dustin."

Dunstan should have known this would happen. He should have known it was too good to be true. "I need to go."

"No," Houston snapped. Dustin heard him suck in a breath. "Don't freak out. I don't know what happened between you and your family, but you want to stay here, right?"

"Of course." But Dustin couldn't. With his father and his brother here, he had to run and do so quickly before they could get to him.

"And you're an adult, which means they can't force you to go anywhere. If you want to stay, we'll make sure you do."

"You don't understand. My father wouldn't think anything of destroying the pack if it meant he could get me back."

45

"I kind of noticed that when he said that I had to hand you over before he burned the town to the ground."

Dustin couldn't breathe. He needed to do something, but what? His father was stronger than him, and he hadn't come alone. Even if Mark didn't want to hurt Dustin, he wouldn't go against their father's orders. He couldn't afford to when he was the alpha heir.

Houston sighed. "Look, I'm taking them to meet Chance in pack territory. We're still at the diner, and they're paying for their coffee, but it won't be long until we're there. You need to stay put. I won't allow anything to happen to you, and I need you to believe that."

"I know you want to protect me, but you don't know my father."

"You're right. I don't know your father, but I know *you*, and I know Chance. He won't hand you over."

Dustin wanted to believe it, but how could he? Chance's first job was to keep the pack safe, and it wouldn't be if he didn't give Dustin's father what he wanted. He couldn't risk the entirety of the pack for one man, especially a man who hadn't been a pack member for that long.

No, Dustin couldn't put all his faith in Chance. He couldn't allow himself to believe he'd be safe when everything pointed to the opposite. He also couldn't wait for Chance to make his decision. If he had to go, he had to do it now.

But leaving meant he'd never see Houston and the others again. It meant he had to leave them behind, even though he considered them family. He couldn't imagine a life without Theo, Wade, and the others, but he didn't have a choice. Unless he wanted to go back to his old life, obey his father's orders, and go through with whatever arranged marriage he'd organized, Dustin needed to run.

"Dustin?" Houston whispered.

Even though Houston couldn't see him, Dustin plastered a

smile on his face. "I'll be fine," he promised.

"Don't do anything stupid. Stay in your bedroom, and I'll find you as soon as possible. Just trust me when I say that whatever your father wants, we won't give it to him. You're safe with us. I promise."

"I know." The words tasted like ash on Dustin's tongue. "I'll be fine. You focus on keeping the pack safe, all right?"

"I will, but Dustin, you have to remember that you're a pack member now. Keeping the pack safe means I'm keeping *you* safe, too. I'm not giving up on you, and neither is Chance."

Just the fact that Houston believed that made Dustin fall in love with him a little bit more. He wished he'd had time to get to know Houston and find out what could happen between them, but he couldn't afford to stay. His father wouldn't take kindly to Chance refusing to hand him over, which meant things would become dangerous for the pack. If Dustin wasn't here anymore, they'd be fine. As long as he stayed, though, it would give his father a reason to attack, and that wasn't something Dustin could live with.

He hadn't expected to be back on the road again, but he should have known better. At least he knew people cared about him. He'd carry that memory when he was cold and hungry.

Houston wasn't an idiot, contrary to what James was convinced of. He knew Dustin was freaking out, but what was he supposed to do? His focus had to be on taking Earl and Mark to meet with Chance, so, unfortunately, he'd have to deal with Dustin later.

The two men came out of the diner, and Houston quickly hung up. He watched them walk closer, trying to understand what they were thinking.

In Earl's case, it was easy. He was pissed that Houston wasn't handing over Dustin without even asking questions. Houston had been startled when Earl had said he'd burn the pack to the ground, but thankfully, Mark was the voice of reason. He'd reassured Houston that his father wouldn't do it, even though the older man looked like he definitely would. Mark was trying to solve this in a more diplomatic way, but Houston wasn't sure it would be enough.

Either way, they were about to find out.

"My alpha is expecting us. Will you follow me to pack territory in your vehicle, or do you want to come in my car?" he asked.

"Mark will drive us," Earl snapped. "I want to know where my son is."

"My alpha will tell you everything you want to know," Houston promised. He was glad that wasn't his job. He wasn't sure what he would have done or said, especially considering how close he and Dustin had become.

He climbed into his car, waited for Earl and Mark to do the same, and drove away from the diner. The pack wasn't far, and no other cars were on the road. It only took them about five minutes to reach pack territory, and when they did, Houston had to resist the urge to head to Dustin's house. Instead, he drove straight to Chance's house, parking in front of it. He'd called Chance after Earl had threatened the town, and the alpha had told him to bring the two men over. He'd been lucky to have enough time to warn Dustin, but he was starting to wonder if that was the best idea.

What if Dustin tried running? Houston wouldn't put it past him, but he wasn't sure how he'd be able to catch up to him. Dustin had a massive advantage — he could fly away. What if he was already planning to do that? What if he disappeared while Houston was busy with his father and brother?

Houston needed to do something to stop Dustin, but what?

He couldn't go straight to Dustin's house because it would draw the attention of Earl and Mark and because he was needed here. As Chance's beta, he had to stand by his side while he faced whatever danger had arrived at their door.

But Chance shouldn't do it alone. Maybe Houston didn't have to be the one to go to Dustin. Even though Theo wasn't Dustin's alpha anymore, he was a friend and someone Dustin considered family. Surely, he'd listen to him.

Houston climbed the porch steps. He didn't have to knock on the door because Theo opened it before he could. They exchanged a worried glance before Houston looked back to see Mark and his father getting out of their car. Mark appeared weary, while Earl was visibly pissed. He believed he was leaving with Dustin, but Houston was ready to sacrifice himself if it kept Dustin safe.

"Dustin?" Theo whispered.

"I called him." Houston couldn't say more because Mark and Earl had reached them.

"I'll take you to Chance's office," Houston said.

"When you're done, can you come to the kitchen?" Theo asked. "I'll get some refreshments ready."

Earl looked down at Theo. "Who are you?"

"This is the alpha mate," Houston snapped.

Earl sneered. "He's a man."

"We're very much aware of that. Follow me," Houston ordered.

He didn't need to ask why Earl had reacted the way he had. He was probably homophobic or some shit like that. That might explain why Dustin had run. Houston hadn't wanted Dustin to go back before, and he wanted it even less now.

The office door was slightly open, but Houston still knocked when he reached it.

"Come in," Chance said. His voice was brusque, which meant he was ready to face Earl and Mark.

Houston stepped aside after he opened the door. "Chance, this is Earl, and Mark, his son. Earl is the alpha of his clan. Gentlemen, this is Chance, the Mayport pack alpha."

Earl walked in as if he owned the place, and Houston had to resist the urge to punch him. Instead, he focused on Chance, who was sitting behind his desk. Houston didn't miss the fact that Chance didn't get to his feet to welcome Earl and Mark. He was sure Earl had noticed, too. It was hard to say, since he'd already appeared unhappy before.

Houston continued looking at Chance. "I'll be right back. Theo is waiting for me in the kitchen."

Chance nodded. "Can you bring me back a bottle of water?"

"Of course, Alpha." They didn't usually use honorifics, but they needed to show Earl that Chance was respected as an alpha. Houston wouldn't have been surprised if Chance's father was either in the house or on his way. He hadn't been the alpha in a few years, but he still helped whenever possible. It made it easier for Chance to feel secure, and the pack was safe in their hands.

Houston left the door open and rushed to the kitchen. Theo was waiting for him, and he made a beeline for him. He grabbed Houston's arm and pulled him closer. There was a tray on the table with a few cups of coffee, and the pot was brewing.

"Tell me," he ordered.

"Those guys are Dustin's father and his brother. They're here to take Dustin back, and they won't take no for an answer."

"They can't have Dustin."

"I agree. I called Dustin and told him to stay in his bedroom, but I fear it was the wrong thing to do."

Theo nodded. "He's going to run."

"Probably, and I can't go to him."

"But I can. Take the tray and go back to the office. I'm going to Dustin. I'll try to convince him to stay, and if I can't, I'll just sit on him until you get there." He hesitated. "Keep Chance safe, all right?"

Houston nodded. "It's my job. You don't have to worry about Chance. Earl and Mark will have to kill me if they want to get through to him."

"I don't want you to die, either. Just be careful, all right?"

Houston hated this. They'd never had to deal with anything like this since Chance had become alpha, and even before, he couldn't remember Chance's father having to meet other alphas in this kind of situation.

He breathed in and out, trying to calm himself as he waited for the coffee to be ready. When it was, he put the pot on the tray, grabbed a bottle of water, and headed to the office.

It almost looked like a standoff when he got there. Chance was still on his side of the desk while Earl and Mark had settled in the chairs on the other side of it. Earl and Chance were staring at each other, while Mark looked like he wished he could be anywhere but here. Houston didn't know what to think of Dustin's brother, but he had better things to focus on right now.

"Why is your beta bringing us coffee?" Earl asked, his voice dripping with scorn and disgust. "You have an alpha mate. That's her job." He paused and sneered. "Although I guess that maybe things are different when your alpha mate is a guy."

Chance wasn't impressed. "Who my alpha mate is or isn't is none of your business. Now, why don't you tell me why you're in my town?"

Houston sucked in a breath. This wasn't going to be easy — or nice.

Dustin had started packing as soon as he and Houston had hung up. Dustin had promised Houston he wouldn't be going anywhere, but how could he not? His father was banging on his door, here to reclaim him, and Dustin couldn't go back with him. He'd kill himself if he had to. If he didn't, his father would find a way to torture him, and Dustin couldn't deal with that anymore. He'd rather go back to living on the streets, even though that life had been hard. At least he'd been free, and he wasn't giving that up.

He pushed a sweater into his backpack, then looked around the room. He hadn't realized he'd accumulated so many things since he and the others had arrived in Mayport. He wished he could take everything, but it would slow him down, and he needed to be fast. His father was distracted at the moment, but Dustin had no doubt that as soon as the meeting with Chance was over, he'd try getting to him. He wouldn't stop for anything, not even the fact that Dustin had become a Mayport pack member. He wouldn't care what Chance said, either.

Dustin's father thought he was better and stronger than anyone else. As a dragon shifter, it was probably true. He'd squash the pack if they didn't hand Dustin over, and many people could get hurt. No matter how much he wanted to stay, Dustin would never be able to forgive himself if something happened to the pack and its members.

So he was running.

He rushed into his bathroom to grab a few things, including his toothbrush, then back to the bedroom and stuffed everything into his bag. That was when he heard voices outside his door.

His stomach sank. Was his father here to pick him up? Had Chance led him here? Dustin wouldn't blame the alpha if he'd washed his hands of him.

When someone knocked on the door, Dustin didn't dare

open it. He stared at the wooden surface, wondering if they were about to break it down to get to him.

"Dustin?" Theo's voice came from the hallway. "It's just Wade and me. You can open."

Dustin's knees buckled with relief. Then, he started worrying again. "Why are you here?"

"To talk to you. Don't do anything stupid."

Dustin couldn't leave through the door, so he eyed the window. It wouldn't be a problem if he could shift and sneak out from there, but his dragon form would never get through. Maybe he could just hang from the frame and quickly shift? That would be a sight—him, hanging buck naked from the windowsill, a backpack around his neck.

The door handle turned, and Dustin realized too late that he hadn't locked it. He'd never had a reason to. He trusted the people he lived with implicitly and with his life.

Maybe he shouldn't have.

But it was hard to be angry at Theo when Dustin knew his friend only wanted him to be safe. That was why he was here and why he was trying to keep Dustin in Mayport.

The door opened to reveal Theo and Wade. They both looked worried, and Dustin supposed they were right to be. But they wouldn't stop Dustin. He had to get out, no matter how they felt. It was for their own good.

So he turned to the window.

He saw Theo's eyes widen, but he didn't allow that to stop him. He rushed to the window, threw it open, and climbed out.

"Dustin!" Theo yelled. "What are you doing? Come back inside!"

Dustin didn't dare look back. He climbed out the window, the cold slapping him in the face. He looked around, trying to find something that would be big enough for him to stand on so he could shift, but the only way for him to go was to the left.

That was what he did. He plastered himself against the house as he finished climbing through the window. Then he threw himself toward the roof on top of the living room. If he managed to get there, he could make it out.

"Dustin, please stop. There's no need for you to do this," Wade begged.

Dustin couldn't afford to listen to him and Theo. They'd manage to change his mind, and it would put the entire pack in danger.

These people had welcomed Dustin with open arms, even though he was a dragon shifter. He'd hidden most of the time, but they'd still managed to make him feel like he'd found a home. He'd even found love for a few weeks, which wasn't something he'd believed he'd ever have.

And now he'd lost everything. That didn't mean the pack had to suffer for it, and Dustin grimly smiled as he scrambled up the roof. As soon as he was steady on his feet, he started stripping. He shivered in the cold air, tensing when he heard someone climb out the window behind him. He turned to see that Wade was halfway through, with Theo holding on to him.

"Go back inside," he told Wade.

Wade's eyes were narrowed to tiny slits, a sure sign he was displeased. "Only me."

"You're going to hurt yourself."

"Because you're not? Or are you the only one who can play the martyr?"

Dustin shook his head. The only way to get Wade back inside was to leave. Once Dustin was gone from the roof, Wade wouldn't have a reason to be there.

Dustin quickly pushed his jeans down his legs, toeing off his shoes as he went. Wade and Theo were hissing at each other and bickering, but Dustin ignored them.

As soon as he was naked, he shifted. Wade yelped, and there was the thump of something falling, and for a moment, Dustin's heart was in his throat. He peered through the window, his long neck making it easy, and found Wade and Theo on the floor. Theo quickly moved toward Dustin, but Dustin opened his wings and pushed himself into the air.

Theo and Wade would be okay, as would the pack. Dustin would keep them safe, even if it meant running away without a single thing to his name. He was leaving everything behind, including his backpack and his clothes. He didn't know if he'd be able to shift back into his human form anytime soon, but maybe that wasn't a bad thing. Maybe life would be easier if he stayed a dragon. Dragons needed to eat a lot more, but as long as Dustin didn't burn too many calories, he should be fine.

Where was he going to go, though?

He hovered over the forest, looking this way and that. From here, he could see Mayport and the houses of the pack members who lived in pack territory.

He didn't want to leave.

He'd never expected to find a home, but now, he had to leave it. Maybe he didn't have to go far, and hiding in the forest would be enough for his father to be unable to find him. The trees were thick, and Dustin had already found a few spots where he'd be hidden well enough that no one, not even a dragon flying over him, would be able to find him.

Dustin wondered if that would be enough to keep his father away from the Mayport pack, but he hoped it would do for now. Besides, once his father left Chance's house, the first thing he'd do was to poke around and see if he could find Dustin flying away. It would be good to hide in the forest until Dustin's father was gone and only then leave Mayport behind. There was a risk someone would find him, but Dustin would deal with that if it happened.

He headed away from the inhabited area in pack territory. He knew more or less where pack territory ended, so he made sure to stay in it as he looked for the perfect spot to hide. Once he found one, he went as low as he could, then quickly shifted and landed on a tree. He was freezing and with no clothes, so he'd have to shift back soon.

He clambered down the tree, relieved when his feet hit the ground. He looked around and wrinkled his nose. It would be a tight fit, and he'd have scratches from the trees on his skin, but it was better than having to go home with his father.

He quickly cleared the space between the trees from any branches that had fallen, then shifted again. He grunted when his side hit the nearest tree, and his wing tangled in some low branches. He had to resist the urge to roar in frustration and freed his wing as calmly as he could.

This place would be his home for the time being. He'd better get used to the cold ground and hard trees.

CHAPTER FOUR

Can you come to my office?

Houston stared at his phone. It wasn't an order, but Chance wouldn't ask him to come if it wasn't serious. It probably had to do with Dustin's family, which was something they did need to talk about.

Everything was a mess. Chance had kicked out Earl and Mark and had told them Dustin wasn't there. He'd had to admit Dustin was a pack member, and Earl hadn't been happy, but thankfully, Mark had kept his father under control. When Houston had gone to find Dustin, he'd learned Dustin had run away. He hadn't gone far and was still in the forest, but all the work Houston had done to get Dustin out of his shell was gone. He was hiding, terrified that his father would hurt him or the pack, and Houston didn't know how to help him. He wasn't even sure there was anything he could do.

Dustin wasn't wrong. His father *was* a danger, both to him and to the pack. Other alphas would have handed Dustin over to avoid a war with the clan, but Chance wouldn't. That put the pack in danger.

Which was no doubt why he was calling for a meeting.

Houston sighed heavily and put his phone back into his pocket. He'd been in the forest, trying to get to Dustin, but it would have to wait. Hopefully, by the time the meeting was over, Dustin would realize that no one expected him to sacrifice himself for the pack.

Somehow, Houston doubted that would happen.

He trudged along the path, trying to find a way to convince

Dustin he should go back to his life. Houston didn't think it would happen as long as Dustin's father was in the picture. But it wasn't like Earl or Mark were allowed to roam in pack territory. They could stay in town, but pack territory itself was out of bounds for them. Houston had followed their car back to Mayport when they'd left, just in case, and people were keeping an eye on them to make sure they didn't do something stupid. Mark seemed more accepting of Chance's words, but Houston wouldn't put it past Earl to try something.

Which could become a problem.

Houston reached Chance's house after a few minutes. He knocked on the door but didn't wait for an answer and opened it. He could hear voices inside, so he left his boots on the porch since they were wet and muddy, hung his coat, and made his way toward the office.

Before he got there, he peeked into the kitchen, not surprised to see Theo at the table, nursing a cup of coffee.

He looked up, and the hope on his face broke Houston's heart. "Have you found him?"

"Not yet. Chance called me for a meeting."

The smile disappeared. "I'll go and try to find him," he said, already getting to his feet.

"Don't. I'll go back as soon as this meeting is over."

"You shouldn't be the only one looking for him."

"I'm not. Do you think I don't know you've been hanging around the forest half your day? We know he's in there. We just need to find him, and we will."

How hard could it be to find something as big as a dragon? Turned out that it was pretty hard.

But Houston had been poking around for a few days now, and he thought he knew where Dustin was. He hadn't taken flight again as far as Houston could tell, which was good, but he couldn't help but worry. Was Dustin eating? He couldn't hunt in his dragon form, and from what Theo and Wade had told Houston, he'd left without even clothes on his back. That probably meant he was stuck in his dragon form and couldn't hunt like that with the trees surrounding him.

As soon as Houston was out of here, he'd go back, and this time, he'd bring food. Clothes, too. Dustin would need both when Houston found him—and he *would* find him.

When Houston got to the office, he found that James and Chance's father were already there. The three of them looked up when they heard him, and Chance gestured at Houston to come in. "Have you heard anything?"

"I'm sure the info is all going to James, but everything is calm as far as I know. Earl and Mark are still in town, making a lot of noisy phone calls at the diner and bitching." That was mostly Earl, while Mark was still a mystery.

Chance grimaced as he nodded. "That's what I've been told. How long do you think they're going to stay?"

"They're pretty sure Dustin is here, so probably until they can confront him. I don't know about Mark, but Earl seems sure that if he talks to Dustin, he'll convince him to go with him and Mark back home."

"And by convince him, you mean force him," Chance's father said with a grunt.

"Probably. Earl didn't strike me as someone who takes no for an answer. We both know Dustin doesn't want to go back, but I doubt Earl cares."

Norman didn't look happy, but they'd already known that. Earl was here because Dustin was, too, and he wasn't leaving without his son.

"What have we been able to find out about the clan?" Chance asked.

Security was more James's job, but that didn't mean Houston wasn't involved, especially since Dustin was right in the middle of this. Still, James knew more, so Houston leaned back and listened.

James cleared his throat and thumbed on his phone screen, clearly having taken notes. "Not much. Looking for a dragon clan in the area hasn't given me any hits. There's no way to know where Dustin is from, and even Theo doesn't know. I can tell you that dragon clans aren't common in our country, and only a handful exist. They're isolationists, so they usually keep to themselves, either because they're afraid they'll be attacked or because they believe they're superior to other shifters."

"And we know why Earl's clan keeps to themselves," Norman grumbled.

Chance nodded. "I have no doubt Earl believes he's superior to us. You should've seen his face when I mentioned Theo. The way he reacted to a same-sex couple might explain why Dustin left the clan, although we won't know until we talk to him." Chance turned to Houston. "Do you think you can arrange that? I know Dustin is terrified and thinks he needs to hide, and he might not be wrong, but we need more information."

"I've been trying to find him," Houston explained. "It's not easy, because he flew toward the deeper area of the forest, but I think I've pinpointed where he is. I can go to him and try to convince him to shift back and come with me to talk to you."

"And you think he'll be amenable?"

"I have no idea."

"Well, I'm worried about him. Theo is, too. It's not right for us to abandon a pack member to the forest that way."

"But he's not wrong," James intervened. "His clan *could* destroy us all if they found out he was here."

"They already know he is. Someone probably mentioned something about a dragon shifter living here and having been seen in town, and word spread. There's no way to stop that, but we can hide Dustin and ensure he's safe until his father and brother are gone."

"But what if they decide to attack? Keeping Dustin with us is too dangerous for the pack."

Houston felt a sudden need to hit James right in the nose.

Thankfully, Chance had his back. "Dustin is a pack member," he said, his voice uncompromising. "We promised we'd keep him safe, and we will. I'm not handing him over to his father, especially since he's an adult and clearly doesn't want to go back with him."

James raised both hands in surrender. "It was just a suggestion."

"You wouldn't suggest we give Houston over. I don't want you to do so with Dustin just because you don't like him."

"I never said I don't like him," James grumbled.

Houston glared at him, but he had better things to worry about. "We need to talk to Dustin," he said as he got to his feet. "I'll go find him."

"Please do, and remind him that he's part of our pack. Even if you can't convince him to come back, at least try to find out more about his clan. If we're going to end up in a war with the dragons, we need to know everything we can."

Houston wondered if Earl was ready to start a fight with the pack. If he was, he knew they'd win, but it wasn't like he could just do it. Humans kept a close eye on shifters, and dragons were in hiding for a reason. The human government would be more than happy to get their hands on an entire clan of dragon shifters and use them in the military or wherever they could stick them without risking an uproar. Earl wouldn't want to risk that.

Hopefully.

Dustin had known he wouldn't be left on his own for long. He supposed he was lucky he'd had a few days, or maybe unlucky. He'd hated being alone, especially since he couldn't shift.

When he heard noises and the sound of someone coming toward him, he tensed. He sniffed the air, but it didn't smell of smoke like it would if his father or his brother had found him. Instead, it smelled of bear. There was no way for him to tell which bear shifter was coming, but he had a pretty good idea.

When the bear appeared, Dustin squinted, but he didn't recognize it. A quick sniff gave him the impression of damp fur and not much more, but thankfully, he didn't have to wonder for long. He wasn't even sure why he had, because of *course*, it was Houston.

The man shifted in front of Dustin and stretched. It had to be cold even for Houston, but he didn't seem to notice. He was fully naked in the forest, and Dustin had to fight hard not to stare. He suspected Houston was doing it on purpose, even though he didn't understand why.

"Hey there," Houston said, crouching over the bag he'd been carrying around his neck. "Why don't you shift? I brought clothes and food. I'm sure you're hungry."

Dustin started shaking his head, but his stomach betrayed him. Just the sound of the word *food* was enough to make it grumble loud enough to send birds flying from the top of the trees.

Houston laughed. The sound was happier than it ought to be, considering the situation.

"Come on, Dustin. You need to shift, and we have to talk. I know you don't want to, but you can't keep on hiding in the forest when we need you. The *pack* needs you."

Dustin grumbled. The only thing the pack needed was for him to leave, but he hadn't been able to do even that. Still, he was curious. It had been a few days, and until now, no one had reached him. Did that mean his father had abandoned his search and left? Or was he still in Mayport, waiting for Dustin to make a mistake? Had he gone back to the clan to plan an attack against the Mayport pack?

Dustin wouldn't know the answers to any of those questions if he couldn't ask them.

He started to move, still unsure whether he was going to shift or try running away, but his wing got caught between two branches. It wasn't the first time that had happened, but the feeling of being stuck and not being able to leave made him panic. He pulled, and one of the branches dug into the thin membrane of his wing. If he pulled harder, he'd tear into it, and he might not be able to fly.

Two hands on his snout pulled him out of his panic. Houston stood in front of him, touching him and looking down at him with affection in his gaze.

"Calm down," he murmured. He pressed a kiss to Dustin's nose. "You're not a prisoner. You're just stuck, and that will solve itself if you shift back. Can you do that for me?"

The urge to flee was strong, but Dustin focused on Houston. He didn't *want* to leave. He'd have flown away if he wanted, but he couldn't bring himself to do it. Besides, he wouldn't have been able to stay where he was forever. It had rained last night, and while he wasn't cold in his dragon form, he hated the rain. He was also starving, which meant that eventually, he'd have needed to shift to eat at the very least.

He sighed, ruffling Houston's hair with the wind that came out of his nostrils. It startled a laugh out of Houston, and he grinned, touching his hair as he did so.

"That was fun," he said.

Dustin didn't know about that, but he reached for his human side and initiated the shift. As soon as he was in his human skin, he shivered, because it was really fucking cold. Thankfully, Houston had come prepared.

He dug into his bag, taking out a huge sweater. Dustin

quickly pulled it on, and by the time he was done, Houston was holding out a pair of sweatpants. Dustin recognized those as his, but the sweater wasn't. It wrapped around him and swallowed him whole, and it smelled of Houston, or at least, Dustin thought so. His nose had gotten used to the smells of the forest, and this one didn't belong here.

"Isn't this better?" Houston asked, a smile on his face as he handed over a pair of tennis shoes.

Dustin stared at them for a moment before accepting them. It was clear to both of them that they were walking out of the forest together in their human forms. Dustin couldn't keep on hiding, no matter how much he wanted to.

Dustin's feet were dirty, but he still put on the shoes. Then he stood there, unsure of what was next. Houston had taken charge, though, and he handed Dustin a sandwich.

"You can start with this. I'm sure Theo will have more food for you once we reach the house."

Dustin shivered in both cold and horror. "Is the pack giving me back to my father?" he asked. His voice was little more than a croak after he hadn't spoken for days.

Houston glared at him. It was an expression Dustin wasn't used to seeing on his face, and it made him feel guilty.

"We're not handing you over to anyone," Houston said, his voice harsh. "Is that why you ran? Because you thought Chance would welcome your father and give you back without even asking what you wanted?"

Dustin shrugged. "I also wanted to protect the pack. I thought that if my father couldn't find me, he'd leave you alone."

"He might in the end, but for now, he's still in town. Why don't we start walking back? I'll tell you what I know as we walk."

Dustin nodded. What else could he do? He'd made his bed, and now, he had to lie in it—or something like that.

He'd known he wouldn't be able to run from his clan forever. He'd hoped he'd manage, but he'd known better. Now, his father had found him, and Dustin would have to deal with that. If he was lucky, he'd have the pack by his side, standing by him and keeping him safe. He wouldn't blame them for giving up on him, though. At the very least, he should have stuck around to explain what was happening. Instead, he'd run, and even though he'd done it to keep the pack safe, it hadn't been the right thing to do.

"So, first things first," Houston said as they made their way through the forest. "Your father isn't getting you back. Chance made sure I knew to tell you that as soon as I could. You're part of our pack, and we'll fight for you if it comes to it."

"You shouldn't have to fight dragons because of me."

"Why not? The pack would fight for me, or James, or even Wade. Why are you different?"

"Because I'm a dragon. The clan could destroy the pack without even trying."

"I'm sure your father wouldn't hesitate to do something like that, but your brother seems to be able to keep him calm, and I doubt either of them is an idiot. What do you think would happen if the humans had to step in to stop a war between the pack and the clan? We're just bear shifters. We come in handy in a fight, but there are hundreds of us all over the country. But what about dragons?"

Dustin slowly nodded. "You think the fear of being captured and locked up will be enough to keep my father at bay?"

"Hopefully. Either way, Chance didn't even tell him where you were. He said you weren't in pack territory at the moment and that you're a pack member, and that was that. I know you're scared. I am, too, because I don't want to lose you. You're not alone fighting this anymore, though. You have your family and the entire pack at your back, ready to step in. You're one of us, Dustin. You need to wrap your mind around that and accept it."

Dustin swallowed. He *was* part of the pack, wasn't he? He was home here and safe.

He had to be.

Houston could see Dustin was still worried. He was, too, but he felt better thinking that Dustin wouldn't be alone in the forest. It had rained yesterday, and he hated thinking of Dustin having to sit on the wet ground with water dripping on top of him. He understood why Dustin had run and hidden, but it wasn't right.

But Dustin's actions had some logic. He didn't want to go back to his clan, and whatever reason he had for that, it was obviously serious. Dustin appeared terrified of his father, which explained why he'd run as soon as he'd found out the man was here. He'd needed to protect himself and also the pack.

That was one of the reasons Houston was hopeful. Dustin was terrified, and there was no way to know how this entire thing would go, but Dustin cared about the pack enough to try to protect it. No matter how much he'd isolated himself over the weeks, it was clear he felt like he was part of the pack. Houston doubted Dustin wanted to leave, and not only because his chosen family was still here. He hoped his presence here was part of it, too, but he wasn't about to ask. His heart couldn't take another scare.

He was startled when he felt something brush against his fingers. Dustin was already moving back, taking his hand away, but Houston would have none of that. He snatched Dustin's hand and linked their fingers together, squeezing lightly to tell Dustin he was okay with this. He'd just been surprised, but there was nothing he wanted more than to walk around the forest holding hands with the man he was falling in love with.

"I should probably tell you why I don't want to go home," Dustin murmured.

"It would be helpful, if anything, so we can come up with a plan to deal with your father, but you don't have to do anything you don't feel up for. If you don't want to tell us, that's fine."

"I do want to tell you. You know about my father now, anyway."

"Why didn't you ever tell anyone else?"

Dustin shrugged. "I was trying to protect them. Especially before, when we still lived on the streets, it would have been too easy for my father to hurt Theo or any of the others in his attempt to get to me. I never would have forgiven myself if something had happened to them."

Houston squeezed Dustin's hand again. "That's why you ran again when your father arrived, isn't it? You're trying to protect everyone, even if it means being on your own."

"Whatever trouble my father is planning will be my fault."

"No. It's your *father's* fault."

"But he's here for me."

Houston stopped walking and turned to face Dustin. He was pale and looking everywhere but at Houston, but that wouldn't do. Houston stepped closer, never letting go of Dustin's hand, and cupped one of his cheeks. "Look at me," he whispered.

When Dustin did, Houston smiled at him.

"You don't want to go back to the clan," Houston said.

"Never."

"And you're an adult. You can take care of yourself, as you proved time and time again. Whatever your father does to get you back is entirely his fault. The only way he's getting you back is by forcing you to do something you don't want, probably something against the law. That means that whatever happens next, it'll be entirely on him. You just want to live your life in peace and be allowed to do what you want. Don't put your father's mistakes on your back because they don't belong there."

Dustin clearly wasn't sure whether or not to believe Houston, but he nodded anyway. That was as good as it was going to get, so Houston quickly kissed him, then pulled him along.

"You're home here," he said, not peering back at Dustin. Maybe Dustin would feel more comfortable talking if they weren't looking at each other. "Chance and the pack will stand by you, and even if something happens and they don't, I'm not leaving you."

"What do you mean?"

Houston swallowed. He'd never thought he'd say this, but he couldn't deny it was how he felt, and Dustin needed to know that. "If Chance decides that standing by you is putting the pack in too much danger, I'll talk to him. If I can't change his mind, then you and I will run."

Dustin made a strangled sound. "You can't do that. You were born here. You're the pack's beta."

"And none of that matters when it comes to you." Houston slowed down enough that they could look at each other. He wanted to take Dustin to his home and give him time to recover, and maybe he should. He'd told Chance he'd try talking to Dustin, but he hadn't said he'd drag Dustin back to him right now. Considering Dustin had spent several days hiding in the forest without eating, he'd earned the right to take the rest of the day to recover, right?

So, Houston stopped. He faced Dustin again, knowing this needed to be said face-to-face.

"Don't get me wrong. I don't want to leave this place, and I don't want to lose Chance, James, and everyone else. This is my home, and I don't know where I'd go if I had to leave. But you're important to me, too. I hope both of us will be able to stay and build a life together, but if it's too dangerous for you or the pack, I won't hesitate to take you away. As long as you're with me, I'll be home."

Dustin's eyes were wide. He was shaking his head as if he didn't believe what Houston was saying, but that was all right. It was a lot for him to take between the time he'd spent in the forest, his father breathing down his neck, and Houston's declaration. He'd have time to wrap his mind around all of that.

Houston quickly kissed him, then took his phone out of his pocket. Dustin blinked at it, but he didn't say anything as he watched Houston pull up Chance's number and call.

"Any news?" Chance asked when he answered.

"I found him."

Chance sounded relieved. "That's good. How is he? Has he tried running again?"

"No. He's fine, even though he's cold and hungry. Listen, I know you need to talk to him, but can it wait until tomorrow? Dustin is shaken and needs a warm shower, food, and a bed. I can bring him to you if you need to talk to him now, but if it's all the same to you, I'd rather wait."

"Just ask him if he believes his father will attack anytime soon. He's already been here a few days, but he's not doing anything, and I'm starting to worry."

Houston looked at Dustin. "Chance is asking if you think your father will attack the pack today or tomorrow."

Dustin shook his head. "It's just him and my brother, right?"

"Yes. We have people watching the town, and so far, it's been only the two of them."

"Then they won't do anything. Even if my father wants to, my brother won't let him. But my dad isn't a fighter. He prefers to let others fight for him, so I doubt he'll try anything.

As long as I stay out of sight, it should be fine."

Houston turned his attention back to Chance. "Did you hear that?"

"I did. Tell Dustin I'm happy he's all right and that we'll talk tomorrow. Oh, and if he could call Theo, that would be great. He's been frantic."

"I'll let him know, but tell Theo to give him some time. The first thing I'll do when we get home is get him into the shower to warm him up."

There was a pause before Chance asked, "Are you taking him home to his house or yours?"

Houston opened his mouth to answer, but he didn't know how to. He'd been thinking about taking Dustin to his own house, but that wasn't where Dustin lived. "I don't know. Dustin, do you want me to take you back home, or would you rather stay with me for a few days?" he asked.

"If it's an option, I'd rather come with you. I know I'll have to face Theo and the others soon, but I'm not ready for that."

Houston nodded. That was perfectly fine with him. In fact, he kind of hoped that once Dustin was in his house, he'd never leave.

Dustin hadn't expected Houston to offer to let him stay with him, but he was glad. He wasn't ready to face Theo and the others after he'd run, especially now that they knew what he was running from. They wouldn't blame him, but they'd be worried and sad that he hadn't felt he could confide in them.

He'd wanted to so many times. Once he'd realized that these people had become his family, he'd wanted to tell them why he was on the run and why he was always so angry. He hadn't allowed himself to because he knew he might have to run at any second, and he didn't want any of them to throw himself into his father's path. They cared about him, and he could see every single one of them doing exactly that. It had been too dangerous, and he'd also been slightly ashamed.

He was thirty-two. What his father wanted or thought of him shouldn't matter, but it did. Dustin's father was the alpha, which meant no one could disobey him. That included his sons. Mark had always gone along, following in their father's footsteps, doing what he could to make him happy.

But Dustin couldn't do that. His father only viewed him as a pawn that he didn't need for anything except to create alliances with other clans. Dustin had stayed for as long as he could, but when his father had told him he'd organized a marriage for him so that they'd be linked to another clan, he'd known he couldn't stay. He'd tried changing his father's mind, but the man was a boulder. Nothing could change his mind when he made a decision.

So Dustin had run. He'd been on his own for a long time, then he'd met Theo and the others. He'd known it was dangerous to become close to them, and he'd been right. Now they were his family, and he couldn't imagine a life without them, Houston, or even the pack. He wasn't sure he'd be able to leave if he had to, and he didn't know what would happen if he didn't.

But that was a problem for another day. Dustin was exhausted because he'd barely been sleeping, and he was still hungry. He longed for a warm shower and couldn't help but wonder where he'd be sleeping tonight. He was staying in Houston's house, but that didn't mean he'd stay in Houston's bed.

But he was about to find out.

Houston hung up with Chance, and they changed direction. Dustin was slightly nervous, but he'd been so lonely and cold, even in his dragon form, that he couldn't wait. Whatever happened, happened. He'd deal with it when it did.

"I'll show you the bathroom so you can shower," Houston

said as they walked into the house. They'd both left their shoes on the porch, and Houston dumped the bag he was still carrying by the door. "While you're showering, I'll put something together so you can eat. Then I think you should go to bed. You look exhausted."

"Thank you," Dustin whispered. He didn't know what else to say.

"You don't have to thank me for anything. I hope you're done running, Dustin. I don't want to lose you."

"I'm not running ever again." Dustin wasn't lying. Either he'd stay in Mayport with the pack, or he'd go back with his father. He couldn't be on his own anymore, but he wouldn't put the pack in more danger than it was already in. If his father brought the clan to the pack's door, Dustin would do what he had to in order to keep the pack safe, even if it meant going back to his clan and marrying whoever his father had chosen for him.

But he didn't say that to Houston. He already knew Houston wouldn't take it well, and he wasn't strong enough to deal with that right now. He didn't know how much longer he had with the pack and wanted to make the most out of it. He wouldn't be able to if he and Houston were fighting.

Houston led the way upstairs. Dustin looked around, curious, especially when Houston pointed out his bedroom. "That's my room. If you need anything, you can come and find me. This is the guestroom, and you can stay here. There's a bathroom, so you don't have to worry about bothering me."

Dustin frowned. He'd expected Houston to want him in his room, but maybe he'd been wrong.

Or maybe Houston did want him there but was afraid to push. Dustin felt fragile, but not toward Houston. He wanted Houston, and he was terrified that if he didn't take this, he'd lose it forever. At least if he had to go home, he wanted the memories.

He shivered, and Houston guided him toward the guest room with a hand on his back. "Shower. Get warmed up. I'll grab a pair of sweats and a t-shirt and leave them on the bed. While you're in the bathroom, I'll go downstairs to get food ready. I can bring it upstairs if you want."

"Thank you."

The shower felt wonderful. Dustin never wanted to leave it, but Houston might be waiting for him, so he didn't linger. When he got out of the bathroom, wrapped in a towel, the sweats and t-shirt Houston had promised him were on the bed, along with a tray holding a sandwich and a bottle of water. Between that and the sandwich Dustin had eaten earlier, by the time he was done eating, he felt much better. The clothes smelled like Houston, and the house was warm. It was easy to feel comfortable here, but something was still missing.

Dustin hesitated, then peeked out the window. It was getting dark, but it was still fairly early. Did Houston have to go out again? Dustin could hear the shower in the master bathroom, and he was tempted to peek in. What would Houston say about that? Would he tell Dustin to leave, or would he welcome him? Dustin had to take the risk. He had to be brave and stop running from this, too.

He cleaned up the bedroom as much as he could, leaving the tray on the dresser and smoothing out the comforter since he'd sat on the bed to eat. Then he went to Houston's bedroom.

Both the bedroom and the bathroom doors were open, so he could tell Houston was still in the shower. He sat on the edge of the mattress, twisting his fingers together as he told himself that even if Houston didn't want what he was offering, he wouldn't kick him out.

He still held his breath as the shower turned off and Houston got out. He could hear Houston hum, and it was so familiar that it felt like home. It broke Dustin's heart. He didn't want to lose this. What could he do to make sure he never did?

"Dustin? Is something wrong?" Houston asked as he strode into the bedroom, wearing only a towel.

Dustin shook his head. "I'm fine."

"Are you sure? Because you don't look fine."

Dustin got up and moved toward him. "I am." He grabbed Houston's shoulders and pulled him down to kiss him.

Houston made a startled sound, but he yielded easily, and Dustin sighed in pleasure. He could do this. He *would* do it, and whatever happened in the future, he'd always have the memories. He'd always carry a part of Houston in his heart, and that was all that mattered.

"The things I want to do to you," Houston murmured, looking down at Dustin.

Dustin couldn't begin to understand why Houston felt that way, but maybe he didn't have to. Maybe he could just go along with it and see what happened. He certainly wanted to. He didn't know what would happen with his father and was terrified of being torn away from Houston, but being with him felt too good.

So Dustin smiled. "What are you waiting for? Show me."

Houston grinned widely. "I love how open you've become, at least with me."

Dustin looked away, suddenly shy. "I know I should be this way with the rest of the pack, too."

"Maybe, but as long as you realize they're your pack, you can behave however you want. Besides, I like that I'm the only one to see you this way. It makes me feel special."

Dustin wanted to tell him he was special, but he couldn't seem to get his mouth to work.

"Want to know what I'd like to do you, then?" Houston drawled, staring as if he could tell how Dustin felt.

Maybe he could. He'd always seen so much more of Dustin

than Dustin wanted him to. Luckily, he seemed to be the only one with that ability, except maybe for Theo, but that was different.

Dustin swallowed heavily and nodded. Houston gently pushed him toward the bed and waited for him to settle against the pillows before climbing on. He came to hover above Dustin, and the way he looked at him told Dustin everything he wanted to do to him.

They hadn't gone far yet when it came to sex. Houston was busy with the pack, while Dustin was busy running. Their dates had been lovely, though, and Dustin had been thinking about this moment almost since the day he'd met Houston. He wanted to give Houston everything he wished for, but he had no idea what *he* was ready for. He was too afraid to give everything he had and was to Houston, only to have to leave him behind to go with his father.

"Now, what were we talking about?" Houston asked as he kissed Dustin's jaw. "Oh, right. What I could do to you. Well, I could tie you up. I could turn you on your stomach after stripping you naked, tie your wrists to the headboards, and spread your legs to put you on display for my pleasure."

Dustin's entire body flushed. He didn't have much experience when it came to sex. No one in his clan had wanted to risk being found out by Dustin's father, and life on the streets didn't make that kind of encounter easy. Dustin could have had quick fucks against walls, and he could have sold his body to survive, but even if he'd done that, it wouldn't have been anything like what he and Houston shared.

Houston was staring, but Dustin didn't know what to tell him. He wasn't even sure he could answer.

"Would you like that?" Houston murmured as he ran his fingers under Dustin's t-shirt and slowly pushed it up.

Dustin allowed him to take it off, and he raised his hips when Houston moved on to his borrowed sweatpants.

"Or we can go to bed and sleep," Houston whispered. "We don't have to do anything if you're not ready for it. I'll be perfectly happy having you sleep in my arms."

It was tempting. It would take care of the turmoil in Dustin's head and in his heart, but he wasn't sure he'd have another occasion with Houston or anyone else. He might be married to a woman in a few weeks, and there was no way he'd share her bed or even be able to think of himself in this kind of position with her.

Houston leaned closer and sucked on Dustin's earlobe, startling him back into the moment. He didn't want to think about what would happen next. He wanted to focus on this bed, Houston, and what he was doing.

Dustin squeezed his eyes shut and tried to get his mind under control. "I want you to do all of that," he croaked. "I want to feel you on my skin and—and inside of me. But I don't know—I'm not sure what I'm ready for. I *want* everything, but I feel like I might break if you give it to me."

Houston's breath hitched. "Oh, Dustin."

Dustin's face was too hot, and he couldn't look at Houston. When he'd left home, he'd sworn to himself that he wouldn't allow anyone to see how vulnerable he was. He'd failed when it came to Houston, but he couldn't find it in himself to regret it.

"Will you let me take care of you?" Houston asked. He gently pressed closer, maybe so Dustin could feel how hard he was.

The towel was still around Houston's waist, clinging for dear life. Dustin could feel all of him, and he wanted so much more. He wouldn't allow himself to break, though, not in front of Houston, not right now.

"Dustin?" Houston sounded more hesitant than Dustin had ever heard him. "I promise I won't hurt you. I'd never willingly do anything to hurt you. I just want to take care of you and show you that I love you and want to take care of you."

The words made Dustin's brain screech to a halt. He nodded before he could think better of it, but Houston *loved* him. He loved him and wanted to show him how much, and Dustin couldn't say no.

And Houston didn't give him the opportunity to do so. He moved so quickly that Dustin almost cried out when his lips wrapped around his dick. Instead, Dustin dug his fingers into Houston's hair, needing to anchor himself to something — and who better than Houston to give Dustin the feeling he needed?

Houston sucked, played with Dustin's body like a musical instrument, and pushed him to the edge. Dustin moved closer and closer to it until he felt like he couldn't avoid falling off. Houston was everywhere around him, telling him how much he cared with his mouth and hands, and it was almost too much.

And then, it was *too* much, and Dustin allowed himself to fall. He clung to Houston's hair, keeping him in place as he came down his throat before realizing that Houston might not want that. Houston didn't seem to mind, though. He hummed as he sucked Dustin dry, taking everything Dustin had to give him.

Dustin shakily smiled when Houston moved up his body and pulled him into his arms. He reached for Houston's cock between their bodies, but Houston shook his head and gently pushed him away.

"You didn't come yet," Dustin protested.

"I don't need to. I'm perfectly happy with what we did."

"I didn't do anything."

"You did more than you can ever understand. But if you really want more, you can do whatever you want with me in the morning. Now go to sleep. You need rest."

They settled under the blankets, and while Houston fell asleep in what felt like seconds, Dustin's eyes were wide open as he stared at the ceiling. Pleasure still thrummed through his veins, but that wasn't what kept him awake while Houston softly snored beside him.

What would happen tomorrow? Would Dustin have to go with his father to prevent a war? He still hadn't apologized to his chosen family for running and hiding in the forest, and he didn't want to leave without talking to them. He wouldn't tell them what he was planning because they'd try to change his mind, but he wanted to at least see them.

He looked at Houston. He was asleep, and if Dustin was lucky, he'd be back before he woke up.

It took a moment for Dustin to wiggle out of bed without waking Houston. Once he was free, he washed up in the bathroom, then threw on the clothes he'd borrowed from Houston and a pair of too-big shoes he found in Houston's entrance.

Then, he stepped out in the night.

It was cold, and he realized he should have grabbed a jacket, but he didn't want to go back and possibly lose the courage to face his family. He wrapped his arms around himself and quickly strode away from the house and into the forest, knowing he'd be back soon.

He was used to the sounds of the forest at night, so he knew the second something was off. He stopped walking, holding his breath as he listened. When a branch cracked behind him, he twirled around, but it was too late.

His father grinned from right behind him. He raised his arm, and Dustin tried to back off, but his back hit something hard and warm. Arms wrapped around him, pinning his arms to his sides, and his father's punch connected with his jaw.

His world tilted, then went black, and the last thing Dustin thought of was Houston.

CHAPTER FIVE

When Houston woke up, the first thing he did was roll toward Dustin. He couldn't believe they'd spent the night together, but they had, and he never wanted it to end. That was why he was planning on asking Dustin to move in with him, even though it was fast. Dustin might say no because he needed a place where he felt safe or a place to hide, but that wouldn't stop Houston from asking. Whatever Dustin's answer was, they could go from there.

But Dustin wasn't in bed with him.

Houston shot up into a sitting position and looked around the bedroom. Dustin's clothes were gone, but that didn't mean he'd run away. With the bathroom door open, Houston could see he wasn't there, but he could be downstairs, maybe getting breakfast ready. Houston had a hard time imagining Dustin poking around the house — it wasn't the kind of person he was — but he wouldn't be surprised if Dustin was trying to find a way to thank him for what he'd done yesterday.

Houston's stomach churned as he got out of bed. He couldn't hear anything or anyone in the house, but he held onto the hope that Dustin was somewhere inside as he went to the bathroom to quickly wash up, then threw on the first clothes he could find. He rushed downstairs barefoot, ready to pull Dustin into his arms, but he wasn't there.

Houston quickly went through the lower level of the house, his hope dimming with every empty room he looked in. Dustin wasn't in the living room, the kitchen, or even the tiny office at the back of the house. Houston briefly wondered if he should go back upstairs to check the bedrooms, but he already knew Dustin wouldn't be there, either.

He was gone.

Houston's stomach churned as he tried to make sense of this. Last night had been almost perfect. It would have *been* perfect if they hadn't spent the night together only because Dustin's father was trying to get to him.

Houston's eyes widened as realization ran through him. Did Dustin's father have something to do with this? There was no way he would have managed to get to Houston's house, but he could have found a way to contact Dustin and threaten him or the pack.

But no. Houston couldn't think that way when the answer to his questions probably was that Dustin had freaked out. He was so used to keeping to himself that he might not know how to deal with what had happened between them. That was no doubt what had happened, and Houston would find him in his bedroom back at the house he shared with the rest of his chosen family. Houston just needed to get to him, which he had every intention of doing.

He was still trying to convince himself that things had gone that way as he finished getting ready. He didn't waste time on breakfast, instead putting on socks and shoes, grabbing his things, and leaving the house. Chance hadn't called yet, but he would soon, and Houston would have to tell him he'd lost Dustin.

That wouldn't go down well.

Chance would find out anyway, but Houston wanted a little more time. He decided to text his friend, warning him that he and Dustin were going to be slightly late. He didn't tell Chance why that was and hoped Chance wouldn't ask. Knowing him, he was distracted with Theo right now, which was good for Houston. As long as Chance's attention was on Theo and not on Dustin, Houston had another opportunity to find Dustin.

By the time he was done texting, he'd reached the house Dustin and his family lived in. The only one who wasn't there anymore was Theo, since he'd moved in with Chance. Houston climbed the porch steps and quickly knocked on the door, bouncing on the balls of his feet as he waited for someone to answer. His gaze went upstairs to the window he knew belonged to Dustin's bedroom, and he squinted as he tried to see through it. The curtains were drawn, though, so he had no idea if Dustin was there.

The front door swung open. Wade squinted at Houston, almost as if trying to recognize him. Houston wouldn't have been surprised if that had been the case, considering how rumpled Wade was.

It wasn't the pajama pants with cartoon unicorns stamped on them or the t-shirt that looked like it had belonged to someone else because it was way too big for Wade. It was the crease of the pillow on Wade's cheek, his bleary eyes, and the way his hair was sticking all over the place.

"Why are you awake?" Wade asked, rubbing his eyes. "There should be a law against getting up before the sun rises."

Houston looked from Wade to the sky, where the sun was starting to peek. "It's the middle of winter. If you waited for the sun to rise to get out of bed, you'd have to stay in bed late every day."

Wade grinned. "Exactly."

Houston couldn't help but smile back. "I'm here to see Dustin."

Wade's expression turned serious. "He's with you."

"I wouldn't be here if he was. He wasn't anywhere in the house this morning, and I can't think of another place where he could have run." Unless he'd gone back to the forest, but Houston hoped they were beyond that. Maybe he was wrong.

He supposed he'd find out soon enough.

Wade stepped back. "You can go check his bedroom, but I don't think he's here. I haven't noticed him around, anyway."

"He's probably overwhelmed by everything that's happening."

"I don't blame him. I'd be overwhelmed, too, if I had a father like his."

"Something tells me your father isn't much nicer than Dustin's."

Wade grimaced. "You're not wrong. Dustin never talked about his father or brother, but they can't be nice, considering what they're doing."

"He hasn't given me details about why he left home and why his father wants him back. Having met the man, I can only imagine you're right."

Houston followed Wade up the stairs, even though he knew where Dustin's bedroom was. It was clear Wade wanted to feel useful and that he was worried about Dustin, too, and Houston didn't have a problem with him sticking around.

But Wade was right. When they opened the door of Dustin's bedroom, they found the room empty. The bed was still made, so it was clear Dustin hadn't slept here. Houston supposed he might have made it before sneaking out, but he doubted that was the case. Dustin's scent wasn't fresh enough for him to have slept here.

Wade put his hands on his hips and looked at the room. "Now what? I thought he was safe, but you don't know where he is."

"It doesn't mean I won't find him."

Wade stared for a moment before nodding. "I know you will. You smell like him."

Houston wasn't ashamed of what had happened between him and Dustin. If anything, he wanted to shout from the rooftops that he and Dustin were together because he was damn proud that Dustin had chosen him, but now wasn't the time to do that.

"Do you think he went back to the forest?" Wade asked.

"I hope so." Because the alternative wasn't anything Houston wanted to think about.

He sighed and rubbed his face. "I have to call Chance. He's expecting us this morning so he and Dustin can talk about his father and why he's here, but it's clear Dustin won't be there."

"Do you think the pack is in danger?"

Houston squeezed Wade's shoulder. "No. The pack is safe and secure, and even if the dragons decide to attack, we have friends and allies. You don't have to worry about anything. We'll keep you and your family safe."

Wade stared at Houston for a moment before nodding. "I trust you."

Houston felt humbled by those words. He didn't know Wade's story, or the story of anyone in their small pack except for Theo and his brother, but he doubted any of them had lived on the streets willingly. He hoped they wouldn't have to deal with everyone's father, but if they had to, they would. Right now, though, his priority was Dustin and finding him.

He called Chance on his way out of the house. His friend answered almost immediately, but he sounded out of breath, and Houston almost teased him for a second. He couldn't forget that Dustin was missing, though. He went straight to the point, knowing Chance would want that. "Dustin wasn't in the house when I woke up, and I can't find him."

There was a moment of silence before Chance answered. "Where have you looked?"

"Everywhere in the house, then in his bedroom at the house he and his family share. Wade hasn't seen him."

"He could have just run again. Maybe he's hiding in the forest like he was before."

"Maybe." Or maybe he'd left.

Maybe Houston had pushed him too hard, and Dustin needed time and space away from him. Maybe he'd decided to leave to keep the pack safe. Houston wouldn't find out where Dustin was until he located him, and he knew exactly where to start looking.

The forest.

When Dustin woke up, his head was hurting as if someone had hit him, so when he remembered that *was* what had happened, he wasn't surprised.

He didn't need to open his eyes to know where he was. He'd recognize the mattress under him anywhere, as well as the smell.

His old bedroom.

He didn't want to open his eyes. He wasn't ready to face what had happened to him and what would happen in the future. He should have known his father would do something like this, though. He'd hoped his father would see reason, but when had he? No matter how many times Dustin and Mark tried talking to him about his most extreme decisions, he always refused to listen because he was the alpha and the one making decisions. The only thing they could do was keep their mouths shut, which generally was the best way to live in peace.

There was no more peace.

Dustin was tempted to stay where he was forever, but when he heard footsteps coming closer, he sat up. He stared at the door, waiting to see what would happen. When whoever was there unlocked it, he scrambled toward the wall, pressing himself into the corner. He made himself as small as possible, even though it wouldn't matter.

Thankfully, it wasn't Dustin's father at the door. It wasn't much better since it was Earl's beta, Stephen, but at least Stephen wouldn't dare hit Dustin.

He stepped in, carrying a tray. His gaze stopped on Dustin, and he nodded, apparently satisfied.

"Good. You're awake."

"You have to let me go," Dustin tried, even though he knew it was useless.

Stephen ignored him. He put down the tray on the dresser, then turned back to him. "You need to eat, wash up, and get changed. Your father isn't happy about you smelling like someone else." He wrinkled his nose, no doubt because he could tell what Dustin and Houston had been up to, even though Dustin had washed up before leaving Houston's house.

Dustin was still wearing the clothes he'd borrowed from Houston, and he wasn't giving them up. "No," he said, his voice trembling.

Stephen blinked. "What?"

"I'm not eating, and I'm not changing. I don't care what my father wants."

Stephen looked like he wasn't sure what to make of that. "He's your father and alpha," he said.

"I'm very much aware of that, and I don't care. He took me away from my home."

"*This* is your home."

"My home is in Mayport. If my father asks how I'm doing, you tell him that I want to go home."

Stephen had never been cruel, but he always did what Dustin's father ordered, so Dustin wasn't surprised when he crossed his arms over his chest and stared at him. "Going against his orders isn't going to do you any good," he pointed out.

"I don't *care*. He kidnapped me and took me away from my home."

Stephen shook his head. He looked sorry, and he probably was. There was nothing he could do for Dustin, though. It had been stupid to even ask him for anything, let alone to let Dustin go.

"I'll have to tell him about this."

"Tell him. I don't care." Dustin very much cared because his father wouldn't hesitate to hurt him if he didn't obey, but he was done bowing down to the man. He'd run because his father wouldn't listen to him and wouldn't allow him to live his life the way he wanted, and he wasn't going back. No matter what his father forced him into, he knew what freedom was now. He could get it back, and while it wouldn't be the easiest thing to do, he knew Houston would come for him.

Unless he thought Dustin had run.

Dustin tried to ignore that as he watched Stephen turn around, leave the room, and close the door behind himself. Dustin rushed to it as soon as the door was closed, but Stephen had already locked it, and it wouldn't open. Dustin sighed heavily, then looked around the room for another exit.

The room was exactly as he'd left it. It was the room he'd grown up in, and it still had his posters from when he was younger. He'd been interested in everything other kids were interested in—space, dinosaurs, and the like. The room didn't feel like his anymore, maybe because he'd changed so much or because he knew that whatever his father was planning wouldn't be good.

He ignored the tray with the food and climbed back onto the bed, eyeing the window. There was no way for him to sneak out that way, since there were bars in front of it, but if things were desperate, he could shift, break down the wall, and fly away. He wouldn't get far because his father's enforcers would grab him, but he was ready to fight them. He couldn't allow his father to pull him back into whatever life he was planning. Dustin had been free, and he wanted that to continue. He'd rather die than be locked up here for the rest of his life or be married off to whatever person his father had chosen for him.

Thinking that way and going against his father's wishes would get Dustin beaten, but he was too precious for his father to kill him. At the very least, his father would try to convince him to give in to his orders before killing him, so Dustin had a little time.

The sound of strong footsteps coming closer made him swallow. It had to be his father, a man he'd never thought he'd see again.

A man he despised from the very bottom of his soul.

The door swung open, and sure enough, his father walked in. He wore jeans and a plaid shirt, and his white hair was neatly combed. There were crumbs in his mustache, and Dustin focused on that rather than on what his father was about to say.

"Why aren't you eating breakfast?" his father demanded to know.

Dustin pressed deeper into the corner, but there was nowhere for him to go. "I won't eat anything until you let me go."

His father's eyes narrowed. "That's never going to happen. I need you to eat and be strong, because the alliance is back on with you home."

Dustin's stomach churned. He couldn't have eaten anything even if he wanted to. "What alliance?"

"The one with the Dagwood clan."

Dustin quickly thought about what he knew of that clan. As far as he remembered, the alpha only had daughters. Not that Dustin would have been happy even if the alpha had had a son. He was in love with Houston, and he wasn't getting married to anyone else.

"What are you giving them?"

His father grinned, but it wasn't a nice smile. "You, of course."

"Which of the alpha's daughters am I supposed to marry?"

"Does it matter? You'll marry one of them, and that's that. I can't have you looking weak on your wedding day, so you'd better start eating and taking care of yourself."

The *or else* was implied, but Dustin heard it.

He licked his lips. He'd never stood up to his father, even when he ran away. The only time he had asked something of his father was when he'd begged not to be married off to someone he could never love, and his father had laughed in his face. He wasn't laughing now, though. He stared at Dustin, clearly expecting him to give in and say he'd do whatever his father wanted.

Not this time.

Dustin sat up straighter. He was terrified and knew his father wouldn't take this well, but he was done bowing to the man's orders. He was an adult with his own life, a new family, friends, and a boyfriend. He wanted to go back to Mayport, and he'd make sure his father knew that.

"I won't marry whoever you chose for me."

"You'll do what I tell you when I tell you to do it. You're my son."

"I'm also thirty-two. I was happy in Mayport. I met someone, and I'm not losing him just because of what you want."

Dustin jumped when his father punched the wall, leaving a hole in it. He didn't seem bothered by the plaster raining down on the floor. He hadn't even looked away from Dustin, and there was no way he couldn't see that Dustin was terrified.

"You'll do what I tell you, and that's that. You won't like the consequences if you don't."

That was all Dustin's father needed to say. He stepped out, slamming the door shut behind himself, leaving Dustin to stare at the door and the hole in the wall.

Dustin didn't regret standing up to his father, but this was far from over. As long as he was stuck in this bedroom, there was nothing he could do against the man.

Nor could he run away again.

Dustin was nowhere to be seen. Houston had been exploring the forest for the past two hours, but there were no signs of him, and he was starting to think that Dustin wasn't there. But if he wasn't in the forest, and if he wasn't home with his family, where was he?

Had he left for the good of the pack? Even though Houston didn't want to admit it, it sounded like the most probable possibility. Dustin had run when his father first arrived, and he'd explained it was because he didn't want the pack to get hurt. It would make sense that he was still thinking like that. He'd given in when Houston had found him, but clearly, he'd only been going along with what Houston wanted. Now he was gone, and Houston didn't know how to deal with that.

He wanted nothing more than to go after Dustin, but he wouldn't know where to start looking for him. He didn't know him well enough, but maybe someone else could tell him where to go. Dustin's old pack knew him better than Houston, so maybe they would have an idea about where Houston should go.

He trudged out of the forest, going as fast as he could. He'd been keeping Chance up to date, even though there was nothing for him to report. Chance knew Dustin was nowhere to be seen, and he'd sent James into town to find out if Dustin's family was still there. Knowing whether or not they were still around might help find Dustin.

Houston took his phone out of his pocket as he made his way toward the house where Dustin's chosen family lived.

There was no text from Chance, so he quickly called him.

"Any news?" Chance asked when he answered.

"No. You?"

"They left."

Houston swore. "What do you think it means?"

"I want to believe they just decided to go because they could tell we wouldn't give up Dustin, but that sounds too good to be true. Have you found him?"

"No, and there are no signs of him. Either he shifted on my porch and flew away, or he was never in the forest."

"What do you think happened to him?"

"Whatever it is, it can't be good, especially with his family gone. Can you try to find out more about the clan?"

"It would have been easier if Dustin had talked to me, but I'll ask around and call some of our friends to find out if they know about the clan."

There was nothing more Chance could do, unfortunately. They knew the name of the clan and who the alpha was, but where was Dustin from? Was it around here, or had his father and brother come from far away?

Houston didn't have those answers, but hopefully Dustin's friends would.

He almost ran all the way to the house and quickly knocked on the door once he got there. The sooner he talked to them, the better it would be. He tapped his foot on the floor, eager to get this over with. If Dustin was out there, having been taken, Houston needed to get to him.

The door opened. Houston blinked, trying to remember the name of the woman standing there. He'd introduced himself to everyone who'd arrived with Theo, but he usually didn't interact with most of them.

The woman smiled. "Josie."

"Right. I'm sorry, but I need to talk to Wade, you, and anyone else who's home."

Josie frowned. "Is this about Dustin? Wade told us he was gone."

"Unfortunately, he is. It would be great if you and the others could tell me everything you know about him and where he might have gone."

Josie waved at Houston to come into the house. "You should sit in the living room. I'll grab everyone so we can brainstorm."

There was nothing Houston wanted less than to sit, so instead of doing that, he paced the length of the living room as he waited for Josie to come back with the others. He was surprised he hadn't dug a trench in the floor by the time they arrived.

Wade was on Houston in seconds. "Please tell me you found him."

Houston shook his head. "I'm sorry. I also found out that both his father and brother are gone, and I'm starting to wonder if they may have something to do with his disappearance." Houston didn't know how they could have gotten to Dustin in his house, but he was going to find out.

Wade paled. "You think they took him?"

"That looks possible, yes. If any of you can tell me where the clan is, we'll go and get him back."

"Why would you do that?" a man asked as he walked into the living room.

Houston narrowed his eyes at Seth. "Are you planning on leaving him there?"

Seth crossed his arms over his chest and glared. "Of course not, but he's part of *our* pack."

"He's a member of the Mayport pack, and that means something. If he was taken against his will, we'll do everything we can to retrieve him."

"Besides, Houston and Dustin are together," Wade piped up. "Even if Chance didn't want to get Dustin back, Houston would."

Houston nodded. He understood why these people were wary, but he needed them to trust him. "Do any of you think he might have left to keep the pack safe?"

Wade frowned. "That's what he tried doing in the beginning."

"But he didn't go far," Josie pointed out. "I don't think he'd want to be away from Houston or us. I understand why he thinks that leaving would keep the pack safe, and he might have left us behind before, but not now that we have a home."

Houston looked around. Several people were nodding while others whispered to each other. No one said Josie was wrong, which made Houston feel better.

But not as good as he would feel if Dustin were beside him.

"Look, Dustin is afraid of his father," Wade said. "He left the clan for a good reason, even though he never told us about it. There's no way he went with them, so the fact that they're all gone points to them having taken him."

Houston nodded. "I agree. The way he freaked out when he found out that his father was here tells me he's afraid of the man and that he doesn't want to go back. It doesn't mean he didn't run to keep us safe, though."

"He ran before because he didn't have anything to stay for," Josie insisted. "Even when he had us, he'd have done it to keep us safe because we couldn't defend ourselves. We can now. We found a home, and the pack will stand beside us in a fight, right?"

"Of course. You're pack members."

Josie nodded. "He wouldn't want to leave us behind. He stuck to the forest when he ran after finding out his father was here. If he's not there right now, it means something happened to him. With his father and brother gone, I'm ready to bet they took him."

"But how?" Seth asked. "He never left pack territory,

right?"

Houston shook his head. "Not as far as I know, but I slept through the night. He could have snuck out without me noticing."

"That bad?" Seth snarked.

Houston wouldn't allow him to get a rise out of him. He suspected that Seth was behaving this way because he was afraid for Dustin, which was a feeling Houston understood and shared.

"He knew Chance wanted to talk to him today. Maybe he didn't feel up to doing that and decided to go home. Maybe it was just too much for him. I don't know, and we won't find out until we get him back."

"What can we do for you?" Wade asked.

Houston looked around the room. "Tell me everything you know about Dustin, his family, and his clan." Houston would find Dustin even if it killed him, dammit.

Dustin glared at Stephen, but he ignored everything else, including the tray Stephen was carrying. Stephen looked disappointed, which made Dustin want to scream at him. He didn't care what Stephen wanted. He just cared that Stephen was doing his father's bidding and that Dustin had a problem with that.

"Not eating isn't going to help," Stephen pointed out as he put down the tray. "Eventually, he's going to find a way to force-feed you. Besides, you'll need your energy for what comes next."

"Yes, because we wouldn't want the Dagwood clan to think I'm too weak to father children," Dustin snarked.

Stephen took his words seriously. "Exactly. They agreed to an alliance because they think they can get something out of it. The alpha only has daughters, and he wants to start having grandchildren. He chose our clan to father those grandchildren, which is an honor."

Not as far as Dustin was concerned. He looked away from Stephen, knowing that nothing he could say would change the man's mind or convince him to help him run. Stephen was Earl's man through and through, even though he wasn't as much of an asshole as Dustin's father.

Stephen sighed, but he didn't say anything else. Dustin heard him retreat to the door, but he waited until the door closed to look up again.

The tray was still there. There was a sandwich on it, which was a good thing because if it had been something smelling any better, Dustin might have given in. He'd only eaten two sandwiches last night and nothing for breakfast, and he was starving.

But he'd rather die than give in. If his father thought he could break him this time around, he'd soon find out how wrong he was.

Time passed slowly as Dustin could do nothing more than look out the window. There weren't any books in this bedroom. He didn't have a phone, of course, and he wondered if boredom would kill him before his father did. He'd rather be on his own than have people come in and out of the room, though, especially when those people were his father. He'd heard him yell before, probably when Stephen had told him Dustin still wasn't eating, but he hadn't come around yet.

He would.

Dustin wasn't surprised when someone neared his door again a while later. It didn't sound like his father, but he still held his breath as he waited for the door to open. He expected Stephen, but it wasn't him.

It was Mark.

Dustin eyed his brother. He wanted to trust him, but he didn't know if he could. After all, Mark had helped their father. Dustin wasn't sure who had hit him in the back of the head, but even if it had been his father, Mark hadn't stopped him.

Mark looked at the tray on the dresser and sighed. "Why aren't you eating?"

Dustin crossed his arms over his chest and glared. "It's none of your business."

"It is when it's pissing Dad off. He wants you to eat and change."

Dustin clutched at his t-shirt. "No. I don't care what he wants or what he thinks he can get from me. He kidnapped me and took me away from my home. I'm not doing this. You'll have to kill me first."

Mark had always been an enigma for Dustin. They'd been close when they were children and their mother was still alive, but they'd drifted apart once they'd become teenagers. Their father had taken Mark under his wing to teach him how to become the next alpha since he was the oldest, and while Mark wasn't cruel, Dustin didn't trust him. Mark had spent too much time with their father, so there was no way Dustin could believe anything that came out of his mouth.

Especially since he knew what their father would do, just like he knew why their father had insisted on getting Dustin back. Mark was very much aware of the fact that Dustin was expected to marry someone he'd never met and that he could never fall in love with, yet, he didn't seem to have a problem with that.

"Do you really consider Mayport your home?" Mark asked, surprising Dustin.

Dustin sat up straighter. "I do. They welcomed my pack and me when we didn't have anyone else."

Mark frowned. "Your pack?"

"People I met while I was living on the streets. We became a pack, and the Mayport pack welcomed all of us. They made us feel like we were home, and we are. They never forced any of us to do something they didn't want."

Mark grimaced. "You should go along with it. How bad can it be? You just have to marry a woman."

Dustin leaned forward. "And father children, right?"

"Exactly."

"How am I supposed to do that when I'm gay? Do you really think I could have sex with a woman enough to get her pregnant? I'd probably throw up just seeing her naked." Dustin doubted it that was true, but he was trying to make a point. "And I have to go live there, right? Because the Dagwood alpha wants grandchildren, which is the only reason he agreed to this marriage. What happens if I can't give him children? Is he going to kill me? What will happen to the alliance between our clans?"

"You can't think like that. I'm sure that if you close your eyes and focus on someone else, you'll manage to get that woman pregnant."

"I don't want to! I don't want to marry a woman I don't know, not just because I'm gay but also because I'm in love with someone else. I want to go home, Mark. If you've ever cared about me, please do this for me. Let me go."

But Mark was already shaking his head. "I can't go against Dad."

"Why not? Do you think he'd try to kill you if you did? You're younger and stronger than him. You could take him in a fight."

"He'd kick me out."

Dustin snorted. "His precious heir? I don't think so. Maybe he'll try to marry you off to someone, make a stud out of you like he's doing with me."

Mark took a step forward but stopped moving when Dustin plastered himself in his corner. He raised a hand, but Dustin didn't trust him.

"You don't understand," Mark said. "You don't know how bad things have become. I'm the only one keeping him in check. He's becoming more hectic, making irrational decisions. He'll destroy the clan if I'm not here to keep an eye on him."

"Then maybe you should let him. Who cares about the clan? Who would want to be part of it when they can't live their life the way they want to and have to bow to an egocentric man? You can't tell me this is how you want to live your life."

Dustin wasn't sure Mark understood how different things could be. He wanted to tell him, but would it make a difference?

"Chance is my new alpha in Mayport," he continued. "He never forced me to do anything I didn't want. He welcomed us with open arms, gave us a house and food, and time to get to know people and truly become part of the pack. He offered to help every single one of us find a job we can be happy with and even pay for college. Dad would never do anything like that. If someone doesn't do what he wants, he kicks them out. He'd never offer anyone a home, although I guess that no one would actually want to stay here if they weren't born in the clan."

"I'm sorry," Mark said as he stepped back toward the door. "You should have known better than to shift where people could see you. We wouldn't have known where you were if you hadn't. I can't do anything to help you. It's better that you wrap your mind around what your life will be in the future and get used to the fact that you'll marry a woman and have to father children. Make your peace with it and make it happen."

Dustin didn't protest. He didn't say anything because Mark wouldn't listen to him, anyway. He watched his brother leave, then leaned against the wall, thinking about Mayport and the people he'd left behind.

It would be easy to believe they thought he'd left. He almost had, after all, but they knew him, right? Even if Houston thought Dustin had left, the others wouldn't let him stay back. They were coming for him. Dustin was sure of that, and it was the only thing keeping him sane.

CHAPTER SIX

They were all going to die.

Okay, so Houston was overly dramatic, and knowing how dangerous the dragons were wouldn't stop him from attempting to rescue Dustin, but it was still terrifying. He'd been close enough to Dustin in his dragon form to be very much aware of how big he was and how sharp his fangs were. Pairing that with the fire he could breathe, the group headed out to rescue him would have to face a formidable opponent.

Hopefully, they were strong enough to make it out in one piece and to keep the dragons away from the pack.

Because they had to think of that, too. What would happen if they managed to get Dustin back? The dragons would know it was them because who else could it be? And they'd come back and possibly burn the pack to the ground. It was enough to make Houston even more nervous, and he looked around the room, taking in the many people he stood to lose.

Chance had convinced Theo to stay back. Theo had reluctantly agreed because Houston had promised he'd do everything he could to get Dustin back. He'd be going with Wade, who hadn't taken no for an answer even though he couldn't do much fighting in his okapi form, Seth, Josie, Matty, Luke, Mateo, and of course, Chance, who had a plan. The first four were part of Dustin's chosen family, while Luke and Mateo had been born in Mayport. It was good to see all of them working together, and Houston liked that this had pulled them together. He just wished they were working as a group in other circumstances.

"You all know the plan," Luke said as he paced Chance's living room. "We sneak in, avoid the guards and every other dragon shifter, get to Dustin, and extract him. Then we sneak out."

"That sounds *so* easy," Seth snarked. "Easy peasy lemon squeezy, right?"

Luke narrowed his eyes at him. "If you're going to be a smartass, you should stay back."

"Everyone should stay back," James muttered. He was leaning against the door frame with his arms crossed over his chest.

Houston didn't miss the fact that he seemed particularly focused on Wade, although, of course, James would never admit it.

"We're rescuing Dustin," Wade said, his tone uncompromising. "And if you can't say anything useful, then you should keep your mouth shut."

James gaped at him, but as entertaining as it was to watch someone shut him up the way Wade had, they had things to do and places to be. Houston stood up straighter, ready to head out. He cleared his throat, and everyone turned to him.

"You know how dangerous this could become. If the dragons find us, they won't be lenient. You all need to be sure of what you're doing. I'm going, but none of you have to come along."

Wade narrowed his eyes. "Shut up. I'm coming, and I know the others aren't changing their minds. Isn't it time to leave?"

It was, so after Chance had a quiet moment with Theo, they headed out in three cars. The tension was thick in the one Houston shared with Chance, Wade, and Josie, and Houston couldn't stop thinking about how many things could go wrong. He hadn't wanted Chance to come because he was their alpha and the pack needed him, but they'd come up with a plan, and Chance's father had stayed back. If anything happened, he'd step up and guide the pack, but hopefully, things wouldn't come to that.

"When are you calling?" Houston asked.

"As soon as we're at the edge of their territory," Chance told him without looking away from the road.

"Do you think he'll agree to see you?"

"I have no idea, but I hope that even if he doesn't, my presence will be enough to distract him until you get Dustin out."

Chance's plan was simple — call Earl, tell him he was there and wanted to talk to him about Dustin, and hopefully distract him. There was no way to know if it would work, and Houston felt awful, having to choose between having his alpha and best friend's back and rescuing Dustin. Chance had reassured him that he'd be fine with Mateo and Wade, and Houston prayed that would be the case. Chance had a microphone on him so the people sneaking in could hear what was happening and be warned if Earl didn't fall for it.

Houston's mouth was dry by the time they reached the edge of dragon territory. They separated, Chance, Mateo, and Wade staying where they were while the others, including Houston, hid the other two cars and got ready.

They moved into dragon territory even before Chance made his call. Houston kept an ear on that and focused on the rescue mission. He could hear Earl snarl something at Chance and Chance calmly responding, then Earl lying about not knowing where Dustin was. Houston almost snorted in disbelief, but they were in enemy territory, and he couldn't draw attention.

"I have no idea what you're talking about and no intention of meeting you," Earl snapped. "You insisted that Dustin is your pack member, which means he's your problem now. You should keep a better eye on your people, clearly."

Houston decided to ignore the conversation. It wouldn't

do him any good to get angry at what Earl was saying, and they'd reached the house they believed belonged to the dragon alpha. It had taken a lot of promises and favors to get the info they needed on the clan and its territory, but they had good allies who were standing by, waiting to find out if they'd be pulled into a war no one wanted.

Luke gestured at the back door they could all see from where they stood between the trees. Only Houston, Luke, and Seth would go in, with Matty and Josie waiting outside and acting as backup. Houston hoped they wouldn't need them.

Luke went ahead because he had experience in the military. Even though Houston was the beta, Luke was the unofficial leader of this rescue mission, and Houston was more than happy to follow his lead.

To everyone's surprise, they managed to get into the house without anyone stopping them. Houston could hear that Chance was still bickering with Earl, and he suspected Earl had pulled his guards to him in case Chance tried anything since Chance had told him he was at the edge of dragon territory. Besides, he probably wouldn't have had many guards in his home. Houston didn't know many dragons, but he had the impression that Earl thought a lot of himself, including that no one would dare attack his home.

"He'll be upstairs in one of the bedrooms," Luke whispered. "That's what I would do."

It took them a moment to get out of the kitchen, where the back door opened, and into the hallway. From there, it was only a few steps to reach the stairs. The house was silent, but they could hear Earl talking from somewhere downstairs, and Houston held his breath as they climbed the stairs.

Everything was going well, maybe too well. Houston should have expected there'd be a snag in their plan.

Luke reached the top stair first and peeked around the corner. He jerked back quickly enough that the hand that shot out didn't touch him, but that didn't stop the man it belonged to. He suddenly appeared, already reaching for Luke again, and Luke threw himself forward. They collided, and Houston looked at Seth, wondering if they should intervene.

Houston started to move, but Seth grabbed his arm. "Give him time," he whispered.

Houston wasn't sure that was the best idea, but as he watched Luke punch the guy who'd attacked him, then swiftly move behind him and hook an arm around his throat, he realized Seth was right. Luke knew what he was doing, and the guy he was now strangling wasn't making a sound. He couldn't with Luke's arm around his throat.

Houston watched as the guy collapsed. Luke waited a few more seconds, then lowered the guy's body to the floor, where the guy stilled. Chance's voice was still going in Houston's ear, so Houston knew that Earl was still focused on his friend and none the wiser about what was happening upstairs in his own home.

"What the fuck?" a male voice said from deeper down the hallway.

Houston swallowed and stepped forward. It was his turn to fight.

His gaze stopped on Mark, who stood in front of a closed door. They stared at each other for a second before Houston moved forward, ready to fight him, but Mark raised a hand.

Houston blinked. That wasn't supposed to happen.

"You're here for Dustin?" Mark asked in a whisper.

Houston didn't know what to do. He nodded curtly and waited. Mark hadn't struck him as being as much of an asshole as his father, so maybe there was hope.

Or maybe Mark was about to call for help.

Dustin could hear the sound of his father talking to someone none too gently in his office. His bedroom was right on top of it, and he'd heard way too much over the years. That was how he'd managed to get away from his father before he was married off the first time he'd run. He'd known what would happen, and as soon as he'd been able to, he'd snuck out and never looked back.

But he couldn't run now. What would happen if he did? His father would go after the pack, and Dustin would never forgive himself.

But could he live that way? Could he marry someone, attempt to give her a child, then deal with whatever happened when he couldn't? He doubted the alpha of the Dagwood clan would take it nicely once he realized there was no way Dustin could give him grandchildren. What would he do then? It was too easy to imagine, even when Dustin tried not to. If the alpha was allying himself with Dustin's father because he thought he'd get grandchildren out of it, he wouldn't take it well when he realized that would never happen. He probably wouldn't hesitate to kill Dustin, if anything so he could marry off his daughter to someone else. The only thing that counted was to make the clan stronger and bigger, and that only happened when children were born. If Dustin couldn't do his job, he wouldn't have a reason to be kept alive.

He nibbled on his lower lip as he thought. So if he stayed, he might save the pack, but he'd probably end up killed. Where did that leave him? Could he put the pack in danger and try to save himself, or should he just accept that his life was over? He might have been able to before, but now, with Houston, he didn't think he could anymore. There was a life out there filled with friends, family, and happiness. Dustin didn't want to give it up without even trying.

He got up from his bed and went to peer out the window. The bars were solid, so there was no way out through them, and the door was locked. Stephen wouldn't help Dustin escape, and neither would Mark. Where did that leave Dustin? He couldn't run from his bedroom, but his father couldn't leave him locked up there forever. If Dustin was going to marry this woman, he'd have to leave his bedroom eventually. Maybe he'd manage to run then.

Or maybe he wouldn't, but that wouldn't stop him from trying. He was done with bowing down to his father. If it meant he got killed, then so be it. He'd die knowing he'd done everything he could to live his life and be happy.

A sound just outside the bedroom made Dustin tense. Stephen had brought food earlier, so he wouldn't come back until tomorrow morning with breakfast. It could be Mark again, but what reason would he have to come? He'd already told Dustin what he needed to tell him. He wouldn't help Dustin, no matter how many times Dustin begged.

So who was it?

The door unlocked, and Dustin decided he needed to take this opportunity. He had no doubt it would hurt because whoever was there wasn't here to help him escape, but he'd try. He owed it to Houston and their friends, but even more to himself.

He plastered himself against the wall next to the door and waited, holding his breath. The door finally creaked open, and Dustin launched himself forward and sideways.

Only to collide with Houston.

Dustin stumbled back, his eyes wide as he stared. Was he hallucinating? Had Stephen or his father put something in his food to keep him compliant? But that couldn't be right. Dustin hadn't eaten anything. He'd drunk some water, but it had tasted fine.

Houston stared back for a moment, and Dustin didn't know what to do. Was Houston real?

Houston beamed, and Dustin's heart raced. A fake Houston wouldn't smile that way, would he?

"Houston?" Dustin murmured.

Houston opened his arms, and Dustin threw himself between them. They wrapped around him, holding him close, and he buried his nose against Houston's neck. He was home, even though he was nowhere near Mayport.

Houston gently rubbed Dustin's back. "Are you all right? Did they hurt you?"

Dustin shook his head. "I'm fine. What happened? How are you here?"

Someone in the hallway cleared their throat. Dustin stepped away from Houston only to find Luke and Seth staring at them. Seth was the next to rush to Dustin and hug him, but Luke stayed away.

That was fine with Dustin since he didn't know him as well.

"We need to go," Luke said. He sounded tense, and he kept glancing up and down the hallway.

"How?" Dustin asked.

"We'll tell you later," Houston promised. "But for now, we need to go."

Dustin nodded and looked around the bedroom. Hopefully, this was the last time he'd ever be here. There was nothing for him to pack and take with him. He didn't want any reminders of his life before he left the clan. So when Houston took Dustin's hand and pulled him into the hallway, Dustin went without hesitation.

"My father?" he asked, keeping his voice barely above a whisper.

"He's busy," Houston said confidently.

"He could hear something."

Houston tapped his ear. "And if he does, we'll know about it."

"He's not the only one here, though. His beta probably went home, but Mark lives here. He might hear something."

"Your brother is fine with this," Houston said as they followed Luke and Seth.

Luke pressed his back against the wall and looked around the corner. Dustin was still trying to make sense of what Houston had just said. "What do you mean, he's fine with this?"

"Exactly that. We didn't know which one your bedroom was or even that you were kept here. We snuck into the house, and your brother found us."

Dustin sucked in a breath. "What did he do?"

"For a moment, we thought he'd attack or maybe call for help. Instead, he told us where to find you."

Dustin's knees felt weak. "My brother told you where I was? But why?"

Houston shook his head. "You can probably answer that question better than I can. He cares about you, though."

"He told me he couldn't do anything for me. He said I had to go along with the marriage, close my eyes and do whatever I needed to do in order to get this woman pregnant."

Seth hissed at them to be quiet, and Dustin snapped his mouth shut. Once they were out of there, they could talk. In the meantime, they had to be careful not to get caught.

Staying silent as they made their way out of the house was the hardest thing Dustin had ever done. He expected someone to jump out from behind a corner or piece of furniture at any second, and he didn't breathe easier until they were out of the house. He was surprised that no one had tried to stop them, but Houston had said that his father was busy, so it was clear they'd come with a distraction. Dustin was dying to find out what it was, but he kept his mouth shut as Houston guided him out of the house, then through the forest that made up most of the clan territory. It was dark, and Dustin had no idea where they were going, but Houston and the other two seemed to know. Dustin trusted them with his life and had no problem following them, even when two figures emerged from the darkness. For a moment, Dustin was terrified and believed they'd been found. Then, he recognized Josie and Matty.

They both touched him as if to reassure themselves he was fine, but they didn't say anything. Their group walked for about five minutes, and Dustin knew they were out of clan territory then. He'd grown up here, and he knew every inch of the place. They were still too close for him to be comfortable, but he already felt better, and it was easier to breathe.

To his surprise, the others started pulling at the bushes. Dustin wanted to look at what they were doing, but Houston distracted him by dragging him into his arms. Dustin was more than happy to go, bury himself there, and never let go.

"I can't tell you how scared I was when I woke up and you weren't in my bed," Houston murmured.

"I'm sorry. I couldn't sleep, and I decided to talk to my friends. I wanted to apologize to them. I never got to the house, because my father and my brother found me." And Dustin's head still ached from that blow.

Houston nodded, his cheek rubbing against Dustin's hair. "We thought something like that had happened. None of us wanted to believe you'd run."

"I told you I wouldn't run again."

"You did, but I wouldn't have blamed you if you had. Your father isn't exactly the nicest person around, and I wouldn't have wanted him to marry me off, either."

"I'm fine now," Dustin promised.

Houston leaned back to look at him. "Are you sure?"

"I am. For a long time, I thought that my father had taken any chance I had of a normal life. It made me so angry that I wanted to hurt people and take out my pain on them. Spending time with the pack and with you made me realize that I have so much more than I believed. I'm still angry, but I know I don't have to be anymore. I'll never come back here, and my father will never be able to force me to do anything."

Houston nodded just as Seth called out, "You need to get into the car."

Dustin blinked, and sure enough, Seth, Luke, Matty, and Josie had uncovered two cars that had been hidden behind the bushes. Dustin hadn't seen them because it was dark or maybe because he was distracted. No one would blame him for feeling that way, but his skin itched, and he needed to get away.

"Come on," Houston said, taking his hand and pulling him toward one of the cars. "Chance will be here soon, and then, we'll go home."

Home. It was all Dustin had ever wanted, and he'd found it in Mayport.

They climbed into the cars, and Houston made sure to hide Dustin in the backseat. He didn't like that Dustin had to sit on the floor of the car with a blanket on top of his head, but the last thing they needed was for someone to notice him as they were leaving clan territory.

Technically, they already had. Clan territory itself wasn't that big, just like pack territory wasn't. But just like Mayport belonged to the pack, the town next to the clan belonged to the dragons. It would be far too easy for one of them to see Dustin and decide they needed to stop him from leaving, and Houston wasn't taking any chances.

Especially with his alpha involved.

He was relieved he wouldn't have to drive and could focus on Dustin and on being petrified. He held his breath until two headlights illuminated the night before them, even though he'd heard that Chance had made it out without a hitch and Earl hadn't agreed to see him. He wanted to climb out of the car to check on his best friend, but he also couldn't leave

Dustin. Thankfully, he didn't have to. Mateo got out of the passenger seat and made a beeline for the cars. Houston quickly lowered the backseat window and leaned out, and Mateo stopped in front of him.

"You have him?"

Houston nodded. "We should probably leave as soon as we can."

"We're ready."

"Let's go. We'll talk more once we're home."

Mateo nodded and went back to the car Chance was driving. Chance took the lead with the car Houston and Dustin were in with Luke and Seth behind him, then the last one following them.

"I can't believe my brother helped you," Dustin whispered from his spot on the floor.

Houston gently touched the top of Dustin's head. "We were surprised, too. When he saw us, we expected we'd have to fight him. We thought he'd raise the alarm and try to stop us, but instead, he asked us if we were here for you."

"And you said yes."

"We did. I decided to take a chance and trust him. I saw him with your father, and I heard him speak, and I thought that maybe, he didn't agree with your father as much as your father believes."

"I don't think he does, but he still didn't help me when I asked him to let me leave."

Houston could hear the pain in Dustin's voice as he explained that. He understood why it hurt. Dustin felt betrayed by his brother, and in a way, he had been. But Houston also understood where Dustin's brother was coming from. From what Houston had been able to see, Mark was doing his best to keep the clan safe, both from outsiders and from his father. The man wasn't a good alpha, but he was clearly still strong enough that Mark couldn't risk fighting him head-on.

Or maybe he didn't want to try. Maybe he just couldn't hurt his father, which would be understandable, even though Earl was an asshole. Whatever the reason, Houston thought he understood why Mark hadn't been able to do anything for Dustin. He hoped that in time, Dustin would see things like he did or, at the very least, that he'd allow his brother to explain.

But not right now. Right now, they were going home, and Dustin needed time away from the family that hurt him so much. If Houston had his way, he'd kick Earl's ass, but he'd have to keep that to dreams and focus on Dustin and making him happy instead.

"I think you can come out," Seth eventually said.

When Houston peeked out of the window, he saw they'd already left the small town behind. They were on a larger road, and even though Houston doubted he'd be able to relax until they were in Mayport, he felt good enough about where they were to gently pull Dustin toward him.

Dustin didn't hesitate. He pushed away the blanket and scrambled into the back seat with Houston, climbing right into his lap and wrapping himself around him. He was shivering slightly, so Houston pulled the blanket toward them and wrapped it around Dustin's shoulders.

His phone vibrated, and since he knew it had to be either Chance or one of the people they'd left back home, he wrangled it out of his jeans pocket and raised it to his ear without dislodging Dustin from his lap.

"Yes?"

"How is he?" Chance asked, clearly on speaker.

Houston looked down at Dustin. "Asleep." Or on the way to falling asleep, anyway.

"I'm not surprised, considering everything he's been through. He needs rest, but I'll have to talk to him once we're home."

Houston wanted to tell Chance to fuck off, but they'd already waited to talk to Dustin for too long. They needed to know everything that happened with Dustin's father. Houston suspected they already knew everything, but he had to be sure. They had to be ready in case the dragons decided to attack.

"Is he hurt?"

"I don't think so. I didn't see any wounds on him, but I haven't checked him over."

"I'll call Theo and let him know we need someone to look at Dustin when we get there. He'll probably need food, too. I wouldn't have eaten anything if I'd been in his place, and even if he did eat, I could do with a snack."

Houston's throat felt like it was closing up. "Thank you."

"What are you thanking me for? I did what I would have done for anyone. He's a pack member. What did you think I'd do? Leave him behind? Abandon him to his father? Even if the man hadn't struck me as an asshole, I would have gone against him because what he did to Dustin isn't right."

"I agree. But it was still dangerous to do this, considering how easy it would be for the dragons to get rid of our pack. Thank you, Chance. You took a risk, and I won't forget it."

Chance snorted. "Just stop talking that way. I didn't do anything I wouldn't have done for every single pack member."

"It means a lot to Dustin."

"Yeah, well, it means a lot to you, and you're my best friend. Did you really expect me to abandon him?"

Houston wasn't sure what he'd expected. Chance wasn't only his best friend. He was also their pack's alpha, and that meant the pack had to be kept safe. That was Chance's priority, not Houston's boyfriend.

"I'm glad to have him back," Chance said more quietly. "He's starting to grow on me."

Houston chuckled. "Don't let James hear that."

"You know he's a big softy under all that snark and asshol-ery. Give him time. He'll get used to having Dustin and the others around. Besides, I'm pretty sure Wade is already work-ing on getting him to soften up."

Houston shuddered. "I really don't want to think about what Wade and James are up to. As long as James leaves Dustin alone, I'm fine with him thinking whatever he wants."

"We both know that's not true, but he'll come around. He just needs to keep us and the pack safe, and it's not easy when we welcome people we barely know and rescue them from their father. He'll soften up as soon as he sees that everyone in the pack is safe."

And if he didn't, Houston would kick his ass.

Chance and James were his oldest friends, and he didn't know how to live without them. He'd find out if he had to, though. He was more than ready to give James the oppor-tunity to show Dustin and the others that he wasn't as much of an asshole as he behaved, but if he hurt Dustin, all bets would be off. Hopefully, James realized that.

Houston and Chance hung up, and the car fell silent. Hou-ston could hear Dustin's slow breathing, and he pressed his cheek against Dustin's hair. He'd thought he'd lost Dustin barely a few hours after finally getting him. It had broken his heart, and fear still lurked there, filling the cracks between the pieces.

But Dustin was back in Houston's arms, and he wasn't go-ing anywhere ever again. If Dustin's father came back, Dustin wouldn't have to face him alone. Houston would stand by his side, as would the rest of the pack.

Dustin was one of theirs now, and they defended their peo-ple to the death, if needed.

Hopefully, it wouldn't come to that.

Dustin jerked awake when the car stopped. He sat up, wildly looking around, expecting someone to be attacking them. He relaxed when he recognized Chance's house, but only for a moment.

"You're okay?" Houston asked, rubbing Dustin's back.

Dustin forced himself to smile. He *was* okay. He just wasn't looking forward to what was about to happen.

But this time, he wouldn't avoid it. He couldn't anymore, especially after the others had rescued him from his father's claws. It was time to be honest, even though it was terrifying. It meant Dustin would have to expose how vulnerable he was to Houston and everyone else who would be in the room, and it would be far too easy for them to hurt him after that. He had to trust they wouldn't, and that was hard, too. He hadn't been able to trust his own father. How could he trust people who were still technically strangers?

But he was willing to try. After all, Mayport was his home. If he had anything to say about it, it would be for a long time, and he wanted to start this on the best foot.

"We can go home for the night," Houston murmured, standing by Dustin as they climbed out of the car.

It was tempting to say yes. Houston would go along with it, even if he had to fight Chance over it. Dustin was tired of running, though. The people surrounding him right now only wanted the best for him. It would be easier to make sure that was what he got if he told them the entire truth.

"I can do this. I'd rather get it out of the way so I can sleep the rest of the night and not worry about what will happen tomorrow."

Houston nodded.

Dustin was pretty sure they'd both worry about what would happen next anyway, but that was something Dustin would focus on later. The first hurdle was to explain to Chance, Houston, and probably Theo why he'd run from his clan and what had happened after he'd been captured.

Dustin squared his shoulders and followed Houston and Chance toward the house. The door flew open, and Theo ran out, throwing himself into Chance's arms. Dustin felt like he was watching a private scene, and he was. It didn't last long, but he almost regretted it when Theo's attention turned to him.

Dustin's friend was pissed.

Theo pointed his finger at Dustin. "What the fuck were you thinking?"

Houston tried pushing Dustin behind himself, but Dustin wasn't afraid of Theo. He patted Houston's arm, stepped away from him, and opened his arms. Theo blinked and threw himself at him, and they hugged in a way Dustin wasn't sure they'd ever done before.

Even though he would have died for Theo and his chosen family, he'd tried keeping them away. It was safer in case his father found him, but it had broken his heart a little not to be able to be as close to them as they were to each other. All of that was over now, or at least, Dustin hoped so.

"I didn't leave because I wanted to," he said gently.

Theo rubbed at the tears rolling down his cheeks. "I know, sorry. I was just terrified something would happen to you. I'm also angry because you never told me about your father and all the bullshit he put you through. You're going to now, though."

The promise that he'd kick Dustin's ass if Dustin didn't was veiled, but it was there. It didn't scare Dustin. Instead, it made him smile, because he knew the reason was that Theo cared about him—loved him, even.

"Why don't we go inside?" Chance suggested as he wrapped an arm around Theo's shoulders and gently pulled him away from Dustin.

Dustin turned to say goodbye to the other people who'd

come to his rescue. Luke had already disappeared, but Seth, Josie, Wade, and Matty were still there, hovering close by. They each claimed a hug from Dustin, and he was more than happy to give them what they needed.

"Don't scare us that way again," Seth murmured into Dustin's ear before stepping away.

"I'll try my best to avoid it, but it wasn't my choice."

Seth squeezed Dustin's shoulder. "I know. I just don't want to lose any of my family members."

"I'm not going anywhere." If Dustin could help it at all, he'd never leave Mayport again.

Once everyone left, including Mateo, who looked like he wanted to ask Dustin questions but didn't dare, Dustin and Houston followed Chance and Theo into the house. Dustin finally allowed himself to fully relax, and he couldn't wait to climb into his bed and sleep for a week. First, though, he had an explanation to give and to beg for everyone's forgiveness for hiding such a big thing from them. Hopefully, they'd feel lenient after what he'd gone through.

Houston took Dustin's hand as they climbed the porch steps to follow Chance and Theo inside the house. Once Theo had closed the door behind them, he took Dustin's free hand and pulled him toward the kitchen. Dustin was relieved that was where they were headed rather than to Chance's office. That would have felt a little too intimidating, considering the circumstances.

"You look exhausted," Theo said. "I'll make you a cup of tea."

Dustin suspected Theo wanted to keep himself occupied, and that was fine with him. It was one less person he'd have to look in the eyes as he explained how messed up his life was.

Chance gestured at Dustin to sit down, and Dustin was glad. He'd been in the car until now, but he was still exhausted. He suspected nothing would help except for a good night's sleep, and he couldn't wait to get it. He'd sleep better once this was over, though, and he was relieved he could stop obsessing over whether or not to tell the others what had happened to him.

"I'm glad to see you're all right," Chance said.

"Thank you. I wasn't sure what to do, and I'm glad you sent someone to save me."

Chance snorted. "Sent someone? Houston would have come even if I'd told him no."

Houston had sat down next to Dustin, and he took Dustin's hand again. Dustin couldn't help but smile at him. He didn't know what he'd done to deserve such a good man, but he promised himself he'd do everything he could to keep Houston happy. Houston deserved it, and Dustin was starting to feel like he did, too.

"I know this hasn't been easy for you," Chance said slowly. "I wouldn't blame you if you told us this is none of our business."

"But you feel I do need to explain."

"If anything, to make sure the pack and you are safe."

Dustin leaned back in his chair. Houston was still holding his hand, and that gave him a strength he hadn't had before — or maybe he'd had it, but he'd needed someone to show it to him.

"I'm my father's second son. The spare, if you will. My brother's always been the first in line to take my father's place as the alpha, which means my father never focused on me. When I was a kid, that was a good thing. I saw how hard my father was on my brother, and I was glad he ignored me. I didn't realize that he'd always had plans for me."

Dustin swallowed and looked down at his hand linked with Houston's. "He didn't hurt me physically or anything. Well, he used to hit me sometimes when I disobeyed his orders, but nothing more. I expected that, considering the kind of person he is. When I left the first time, it was because he told me I was set to marry someone. He'd always said he'd rather have had a girl, and I didn't understand why until he told me about the arranged marriage. It would have been easier if I were a woman, but he managed to ally himself with another clan even though I'm not. I was supposed to marry that alpha's daughter and give her children. From what I know, the Dagwood alpha only has daughters. I suppose he views them like my father does, but he also needs an heir. Clearly, this was the best way for both clans to get what they wanted."

"But you didn't want to marry a woman," Theo said as he placed a steaming mug in front of Dustin before sitting next to him.

"I've never liked women that way. I told my father, thinking he'd cancel the wedding, but he didn't. He never cared what I wanted or how I felt. So I ran. I lived on the streets for a while, then I met Theo, and we came here. When my father came here, I knew he was here to get me back and marry me off. I wanted to run to keep the pack safe, but I couldn't anymore. I was tired. I still am, and I don't want to lose everything again because he's a stubborn asshole. Still, I would have gone with him willingly if it meant keeping the pack safe. I don't know how he's going to react to what happened tonight, but eventually, he'll understand I'm here, and he'll take his revenge out on the pack."

Once again, Theo took Dustin's empty hand. He squeezed tightly, and he didn't let go. He and Chance looked at each other, then they both turned their attention to Dustin.

"Whatever happens next, you're a pack member," Chance explained. "We'll always come for you."

And for the first time, Dustin believed it.

CHAPTER SEVEN

Houston laughed and pulled Dustin deeper into the forest, following one of the cubs running ahead of them.

"I'm still not sure that putting me in charge of this was a good idea," Dustin muttered.

"Why not?"

"I could hurt one of them. I don't know what to do with children."

"From what I saw, you're perfect with them. They also feel safe with you, which is a plus."

Dustin's cheeks flushed, making him even more beautiful. Houston knew he was uncomfortable taking care of the children, but he'd graciously accepted when Chance had suggested it. They'd all agreed that it was better for him to avoid the town as much as he could, at least until they were sure his father wouldn't come for him. It wasn't great, and maybe Dustin truly was uncomfortable with the kids, but he took care of them as if they were his own, and more than once, Houston had wondered what it would be like for them to have kids.

It was too soon, and he wasn't about to ask Dustin, but he could see it happening. Now that he and Dustin were living together, he couldn't wait to see what would happen next. Their future was bright, even with the shadow of Dustin's father hovering over him.

But that was all he was. Dustin's father hadn't contacted them again, and Houston had wondered if maybe, he hadn't realized they'd been the ones to take Dustin. It sounded improbable, especially since Chance had been there to distract him that night, but maybe the man wasn't as smart as Houston had believed.

Either way, Dustin had been left alone, and he'd finally started to relax. He was blooming with the pack making him feel like he belonged, and the fact that the mothers trusted him enough to leave their cubs in his hands had touched him, even though he still complained about it. Houston had started coming by the small daycare daily to help, but Dustin didn't need him to. He'd protested, but he knew what he was doing.

They played hide and seek with the cubs, some in their human form, others in their bear form, until it was time to go home. It took a moment to gather all the children. Then they corralled them back to the daycare, where their mothers were already waiting. Dustin spoke to a few of them, and Houston couldn't look away. No matter what Dustin said or his anger issues, he was made for this. Besides, he hadn't snapped at anyone since he'd come back from clan territory, and Houston suspected he'd been angry before because of how his father had treated him. Now that he was happy and felt safe, he didn't have a reason to get angry at people or to shift to scare them.

Once everyone was gone, Dustin leaned against Houston's side. Houston wrapped an arm around his shoulders, but his phone rang just as he was about to ask Dustin if he was ready to go home.

Houston sighed and dug it out of his pocket.

"Work?" Dustin asked as they started walking toward their home.

"I don't know. It *is* Chance, though." Houston raised the phone to his ear as he answered. "Hey, boss."

Normally, the teasing would have made Chance chuckle, at the very least. He was serious now, though. "Are you with Dustin?"

"Yes."

"I need both of you to come to my office."

"Is everything all right? Is it Dustin's father?"

"In a way. No one is in danger, but I need you here."

It was good that Chance had reassured Houston before Houston could freak out. "We're just leaving the daycare, so we'll be there soon."

"Good."

Dustin looked worried, so Houston quickly reassured him. "He said everyone is fine, so try not to worry too much."

Dustin smiled, but he didn't look convinced. "How can I not worry when I know my father's still out there, probably trying to find a way to get to me?"

"No matter how hard he tries, he'll never get you. You're a Mayport pack member, remember?" And even more importantly, he was Houston's.

Instead of going home to cuddle and spend the rest of the day together, they rushed to Chance's house. Theo was waiting for them when they arrived and quickly waved them in. Houston could hear the sound of Chance talking to someone in his office. He tensed, but he tried not to let it show. Chance wouldn't put Dustin in danger, and he'd never agree to have Dustin's father come into pack territory again.

"Is he with someone?" he asked Theo.

Theo shook his head. "On the phone. You need to go in."

Houston was getting even more worried, but he'd never let Dustin do this alone, so they both walked into Chance's office. Sure enough, Chance was behind his desk, talking on the phone, but he gestured at them to sit down. Then, he lowered his phone and touched something on the screen. "Your son is here," he said. His uncompromising tone made sense when Houston realized he was talking to Dustin's father.

"How could you do this to your clan?" Earl's voice boomed over the phone.

Dustin looked lost. "Do what? Leave? How could you do all you did to me? How could you try to force me to marry someone I could never love?"

"That's not what I'm talking about! Don't play innocent, because we both know you're not. You attacked the clan. Your *pack* did, no matter what you and that alpha of yours are saying."

Houston looked at Chance in question, but Chance opened his hands and raised his shoulders, silently telling Houston he had no idea what Earl was talking about.

"The clan was attacked?" Dustin asked, sounding as bewildered as Houston felt.

"As if you don't know that."

"Can you assume we don't have any idea what you're talking about and explain what happened?" Chance intervened.

There was a moment of silence before Earl started speaking again. "We couldn't shift. We were attacked last night and lost so many people that the clan is barely a clan anymore."

"Is Mark okay?" Dustin asked, his voice trembling.

"He's gone."

Dustin gasped, and Houston turned his entire attention to him. He opened his arms, and Dustin climbed into his lap, burying his face against his neck. No matter how angry Dustin was, Mark had still been his brother. They'd been close when they were children, and now, they've never had the opportunity to make up and find a way to be in each other's lives as adults.

"You said you couldn't shift," Chance said.

"We tried, but none of us could. It made it easy for the attackers to kill as many dragons as they could."

"We had nothing to do with any of this. The fact that you couldn't shift points to someone else."

"The clan doesn't have enemies."

Houston begged to differ, but it wouldn't help to tell Earl

how much he hated him. "When will you hold Mark's funeral?" he asked instead. He was thinking about who could take away the ability of an entire clan to shift, and the only thing he could come up with was the old stories of magic.

Earl didn't even ask who was talking. "We can't find his body, so there will be no funeral. Besides, with so many dead, it would be impossible to have one for everyone. You won, Dustin. You wanted to be free and for the clan to disappear, and you got it. Stay away from us. Don't ever come back because this isn't your home anymore."

Earl hung up, and Houston squeezed his arms tighter around Dustin.

"He didn't say Mark was dead," Chance pointed out.

"You think he's still alive?" Dustin asked.

Houston didn't want to give him false hope, but it was a possibility. He wanted it to be true.

"He might be," Chance said. "And maybe he'll come to you. We'll have to wait to find out."

"What about the clan?"

"You heard your father. He won't come after you again, which means the pack is safe. The clan has been decimated from the sound of it, so we won't have to be afraid of them anymore. You can finally relax, although I'm sorry this happened to the clan."

Dustin shook his head. "I'm only sorry about Mark."

"Well, if he finds his way to us, we'll welcome him. But you're safe now, Dustin."

Dustin relaxed against Houston's chest. Things had gone the right way for them, but Houston still wished they hadn't happened the way they had. Dustin was worried about his brother, but there was no way for them to find out what had happened to Mark. They had to wait for Mark to reach out to them, and he might never do it.

But Dustin wouldn't have to worry about whatever

happened next with the dragons. He was home with the pack, in Houston's arms and his heart, and that was all Houston had wanted.

ABOUT THE AUTHOR

Catherine is the creator of several series, most of them paranormal, including the Whitedell Pride Series and the Gillham Pack Series. While she graduated in translation, she decided to go the writer's way because it was more fun to create her own stories and characters.

She's been living in Italy for more than twenty years, but she's a daughter of the North—Belgium to be precise—and she misses it so much that she's already planning to move back.

She loves pizza—probably too much—her son, her pets, and of course, books. She sneaks some reading time into her schedule every time she has five minutes free from writing, demands from her various pets and son, and lastly, housework.

Connect with her:

lievens.catherine@gmail.com
BookBub: https://www.bookbub.com/authors/catherine-lievens
Website: https://authorcatherinelievens.com/
Facebook: https://www.facebook.com/catherine.lievens.9
Facebook Group: https://www.facebook.com/groups/411788002341528/
Twitter: https://twitter.com/authorCLievens
Newsletter: http://eepurl.com/c-uvKn

www.ingramcontent.com/pod-product-compliance
Lightning Source LLC
Chambersburg PA
CBHW060634130626
46555CB00002B/793